Contin Farm

Book One: Powerless

A. J. Bissett

ISBN: 069282409X
ISBN 13: 9780692824092

Chapter 1

Barbara Walters

Three hours west of Fort Worth, Texas

Tuesday, March 2015, 5:19 p.m.

My anxiety surges when the bright little gasoline symbol lights up, since gas stations out here are sparse.

It haunts me like a glowing swastika, an unwanted reminder of my irresponsible decision to not fill up thirty miles ago, when I had the chance. But the light wasn't on then, so why waste the money?

I seem to do this a lot, hoping a miracle will prolong my tank or I'll suddenly have a full-time chauffeur appear, so the gas money really would have been wasted. I prefer to wait until I'm on fumes to take it seriously, which works in the city but not in a farming town off an FM or RM highway in Texas.

The descending sun's vastness occupies one of my three views, the others being the two-lane highway in front of me and the rolling plains surrounding me. Road tripping alone is boring, especially without a phone and my personal road-trip playlists. I haven't heard a full song since I left Fort Worth, just scanned clips on the radio struggling to stay in reception, consisting of Tejano, autotuned country, classical, and talk radio.

I pass a longhorn as bored as me, with beady eyes and a look of fatigue, watching the travelers go by on his highway. To pass the time, I pretend I'm being interviewed by Barbara Walters to talk about addiction and codependency.

"So what, Poppy, propelled you to get sober at the young age of twenty-one? Was there anyone in your life, any codependents that were giving you money for drugs and alcohol, or did you have anyone in your family who begged you to get soba?"

"No, not at all. It was more me begging me to get sober. Addiction is a constant war you have in your mind: Do I stop, or do I try again? Do I stop or try again? But this shitty thing happened to me today, so do I *really* stop or try again? Okay, I can't stop for too long, so I'll try to stop longer. Okay, not good at that, so fuck it. I'll just keep the train moving until I'm *really actually* ready to stop."

"Fascinating."

"When I realized I would always be in the battle with alcohol and Xanax, I knew I needed to change. I actually went to rehab with the intentions of learning some new tricks for how to have two, since I was always unsuccessful at that." In my mind, Barbara looks confused.

"Twicks to drink a couple?"

"Yeah. Like if you're a showgirl or a pageant queen, you have the Vaseline trick to keep smiling, or the teacher trick where you make your students think they have a say as to what they'll be learning when really you have the lesson already planned. You just hype them up about it."

"I see."

"I really wanted rehab to teach me how to only want a drink or a half a milligram of Xanax. I had no idea there were people who actually didn't drink in the world. I thought people were lying at meetings when they stood up to tell everyone they had ten to twenty years. I rolled my eyes every time. I wasn't aware that I, of all people, could be an alcoholic or a drug addict. I was so naïve. I thought meetings were for people to comfort you when you came in hungover, or to listen to your story from the night before."

"So you thought you were special?" Barbara asks.

"Yep. In my mind I was too young, too pretty, too educated, or basically too privileged to be an alcoholic, but to answer your question, I never had any issues with codependents. I was in college, and that's just what people did. I didn't know it was a questionable act to sip on a minibottle of wine in jewelry-making class between soldering jump rings with a torch when the teacher wasn't looking if I wanted some wine. To me I just thought I liked wine. It was news to me to learn that it was abnormal to always want to change how I was feeling."

"So that's what you felt, Poppy, even though you lived in a nice place in Nob Hill in San Francisco. You had the trolley car taking you to class and had the luxury of your successful parents footing the bill, yet you were always trying to change how you felt?" She looks disgusted.

"Yes, Barbara. Nothing is good enough for addicts and alcoholics when they're in the blurry midst of addiction. There's no amount of this or that on the exterior that keeps an alcoholic away from a drink or an addict from a drug. My outside circumstances had no effect on my internal struggle to stay sober long enough to do my homework, laundry, shower, go to class or a social event. By that point I'd be too wasted and just wanted to stay home because I was 'tired,' when really I was isolated. I had all I wanted alone in my studio, yet I was miserable being alone. In class, I would try to convince my acquaintances to take a shot with me during our ten-minute breaks. I was annoyed that no one wanted to party like I did, and didn't understand it. I thought they were all boring and pretentious and missing out on life."

Barbara shakes her head slightly and places her hand under her chin. "Did your college friends ever say anything to you about it? Were they at all concerned?"

"No. I mean, I'm sure they thought I was a little extreme and passionate or whatever, but they were all from California and New York and Europe, so they were used to the crazy. I'm sure they knew better to say anything to me about it until I was ready to make the connection that I couldn't stop once I started and I couldn't stop starting. When the alcohol, weed, and Xanax stopped working and I looked at my gay Jewish friend and told him I didn't know if I should drink or take a pill and he told me that I probably shouldn't do either, I couldn't comprehend that. My mind was blown. That wasn't an option."

"Which part blew your mind?"

"That I shouldn't do either. I had no idea that people sat in their own boredom or anxiety. I couldn't rationalize that if you were uncomfortable, why wouldn't you change how you felt with a drink or drug? To me that response to life was the only one that worked…until it didn't anymore."

"And what about your parents? Did they think there was a problem?"

"Well, they knew I was in college, but they weren't aware I was taking Xanax and drinking in absurd volumes, but I didn't realize it was absurd until later."

"And how much would you drink?"

"Um, I really don't remember. I feel like I would easily put a bottle of wine away, then get the craving for more because the allergy had gone off, and then I'd switch to screwdrivers. It's funny: I never wanted to always get hammered, or else I would have started the night with straight vodka, if getting wasted was my intention. That's one way to tell if you're an alcoholic or an addict: how drunk you get whenever you drink. Most of us didn't go into the night thinking, 'Let's go out tonight and get super drunk or high.' It's just something that happens, whether we want it to or not."

"Interesting," Barbara says. "Didn't you say your dad was in recovery?"

"Yeah, he is. I think he's been clean for, like, thirty-something years. There's nothing he could have done to convince me, though, if that's what you mean. If he would have known the quantities I drank or that I was taking Xanax every day, I'm sure he wouldn't pay my rent or give me any money. He's knows that being an active alcoholic or an addict shouldn't be a comfortable, cushy lifestyle. If it is, then someone's doing the addict an extreme disservice. Homelessness, poverty, jail time, prostitution, hunger, panhandling—all come along with being a drug addict or alcoholic. Those are the lifestyle decisions we make in order to maintain our habit. It isn't an easy life, and it shouldn't be. People who make it any easier for addicts are contributing to their demise."

"Interesting. So you believe…that by giving the addict a place to stay or money for gas or food, they're actually doing the wrong thing by helping them?" Barbara asks, looking at her notecards.

"One hundred percent yes, if they are the real addict or alcoholic, Barbara. It's an internal dialogue addicts need to have with themselves. No amount of convincing, guilt-tripping, or 'talking sense into' an addict will work, because no human or object can remove their obsession. A spiritual entity or a power greater than them is the only thing that can remove their problem."

"So seeing a counselor or going to rehab doesn't help?" Barbara asks, tilting her head.

"Well, yes, of course, and don't get me wrong: those are wonderful things, but they're not enough to keep the addict sober, because addiction is not a knowledge problem. It's a spiritual problem. The only knowledge the addict needs to know is, can they or can't they stop once they start, comfortably?"

"Fascinating. So what then, Poppy, should a parent or loved one do if they are faced with the devastating battle with an addict when they can't get the addict to see how they're hurting others?"

"Well, they need to understand that they can't solve the problem for them. The addict needs to figure it out on their own, start taking some initiative and responsibility for their actions, and stop blaming people and circumstances, whatever they are. Also, don't give them money. Giving an addict money is like giving a kid with a peanut allergy a jar of Jif and simultaneously lecturing him on how he needs to get help, and can't he see how it hurts him and us to eat the peanut butter?"

Barbara takes a sip of water and adjusts her posture.

"Or I see a lot of parents with addicted daughters who feel powerless and worry about her safety and think, 'If we don't give her the money for drugs, then she will either steal or become a prostitute.' But the funny thing is, Barbara, their kid has a far greater chance of overdosing with the money her parents gave her versus being murdered while prostituting. Maybe her giving happy endings to nasty, fat, middle-aged men who smell like cat pee and cheap wine will make her realize how dire her situation is, and she will want help faster because inside she knows what she's doing is eating her soul alive since she had aspirations to be a teacher, nurse, or social worker."

"Powerful stuff," Barbara says. I look back at my dashboard. I still need a gas station.

"Or let's hypothetically say you see your three-year-old addict who's addicted to running across the highway by himself. One time he squirms away from your arms and is headed for the highway in rush-hour traffic. Hopefully, you'd run as fast as you could to stop him and say something like, 'Don't *ever* do that again. Do you understand me? That's a quick way to die when someone's tire rolls over your head and crushes your skull!'"

Barbara has a look of shock.

"But Barbara, if you're giving an addict a place to sleep, food to eat, or especially cash, you're saying to the toddler, 'Just be careful, all right? Try not to get hit by cars, but you seem to know what you're doing, so I bought you some new Nikes and a bottle of water so you'll be hydrated. Remember, if you make it out alive, you'll always have a place to stay if you would like to try it again tomorrow.'"

I pop open my Red Bull. This is going to be a long drive to El Paso.

Chapter 2

Tyler

Tyler, Texas

1993

I am six years old, sitting in the back seat of my dad's Corolla with my bouncy, chatty older sister on our way to our grandparents' plantation home in Shreveport, which I've visited several times prior. Then they'll come. With familiar scenery to cue them, I will almost certainly get them when I watch the blur of the trees fly by the back seat window, smearing shades of hunter green and brown through my mind. I'll then be mentally taken over by my own brain, afraid of my own mental capacity, or lack thereof.

If I see or hear specific things on the road trip (usually fir trees, the sound of the highway, a particular shade of blue), what will follow is a powerless, anxiety-fueled, gut-wrenching feeling that I am somehow reliving the same road trip year after year. I know that I wear the same bow, slightly pulling on my ash-blond hair, the same shoes and dress, have eaten the same lunch as I did last year, and can even taste it.

I feel for about a minute I am having flashbacks, rewinding and reliving my own life like a human VCR, unaware that the experience of doing so isn't normal. Lastly a euphoria hits, sometimes making the horrifying situation bearable because for about three minutes, I love everything and everyone. I want to sing with the birds, play with my family, and tell them I love them. I feel lighter, refreshed, as if my brain had just woken up from a dream, and I am ecstatic to be mentally back in the present moment in my dad's Corolla with my annoying sister.

A bizarre memory of a Dalmatian sitting patiently in my grandparents' neighbor's yard, wagging its tail in anticipation for me to come play, flashes through my mind frequently. A Dalmatian in their neighborhood never existed, but the memory of one always comes back (usually triggering an episode), as though my brain desperately wants to claim a memory of something that didn't happen or exist. Lacking the adequate vocabulary as a six-year-old to explain to my parents my brain is flipping inside out or swimming away keeps me at a disadvantage. I guess they just assume I am a little quirky and whatever I am experiencing is normal.

Chapter 3

New Orleans, 2015

I heard about this world-famous psychic, Wanda, years before. She appears on talk shows and gives interviews about her life as a clairvoyant, as well as reality shows about paranormal activity. I have been fascinated by her career for years, so when I get an appointment with her while I am visiting friends in New Orleans, I am thrilled. She works in an office like normal folk, with a desk and a computer. Most psychics, in my mind, work out of studios that smell like incense and have velvet furniture and dream catchers. Her first question to me is about my father. "Is he really super smart, like…brilliant?" I roll my eyes.

"Um, he's okay. Owns his own company and survived the great recession. If you asked him, he would definitely think so."

She tells me about my maternal grandfather, whom I've never met (nor has my mother). He died in random circumstances before I was born, and there was a debate whether he was murdered or committed suicide. Wanda tells me he was too cocky to commit suicide, but she suspects foul play by someone whose name starts with a *C*. My mom says the *C* belonged to his brother-in-law, Cricket, and they notoriously feuded for years. One day Cricket had enough and put an end to my sharp-tongued grandfather.

I've gone to see Wanda about these mysterious attacks I've been having, how they are progressively getting worse, and how powerless I've felt since the doctors don't believe it is any cause for concern. I am out of patience and need something other than a doctor who isn't interested in my personal concern for my livelihood as much as shoving the newest pill down my throat for anxiety, depression, or bipolar disorder.

It's unfortunate that throughout our childhood we're taught that all doctors are here to help because they're the only ones with all the answers, but what happens if they're *not* or *don't*? What happens when you temporarily feel better but end up spinning into an emotional roller coaster of addiction, refills, and withdrawal aches and pains? Out to keep you coming back, doctors prescribe an array of benzodiazepines, amphetamines, and pain medications of assorted colors and strengths because you're a little more anxious than usual, have trouble focusing, or got your wisdom teeth pulled. We're given tasty doses potent enough to put a stallion to sleep in orange cylinders that rest comfortably in the palm of your hand so you can grip them tightly, like an infant gripping the fingers of an adult for comfort and stability. We do the same things now as when we were newborns, only the comfort comes from orange plastic instead of peachy flesh.

"El Paso," Wanda says clearly.

"What?"

"You need to go to El Paso. For some reason I'm picking up something that tells me the doctor you need is there. Have you been there before?"

"Yeah, just passing through. Nothing special."

"Well, you need to go back," she says, looking me square in the eye. When I fly back into Dallas, I immediately prepare myself for my next road trip.

Max moved to Dallas from Wisconsin to live at the Bryant House, a sober-living residence in the downtown area. It looks strange to date or be interested in someone in sober living, but I can't help but be drawn to his eyes, voluminous hair, and James Dean style. I miss his tattoo sleeves, which he grips the sheets with when he pulls in my naked body. He bartends at a neighborhood bar in Dallas; the answer to whether a recovering drug addict can bartend remains to be seen, but if he's working his program, he can have any job he wants. Currently he's in a Tommy Lee phase. A few months ago, he decided he wanted to be a ranch hand and buy livestock and a few pairs of boots. Before that he contemplated going back to school to get his law degree. Changing interests is something extremely common to newly sober folks, but I'm thrilled with his most recent musician phase. He started playing the drums and revisited his guitar again, something he is genetically predisposed to be successful at, but he decided he was done with music for good after he got sober.

Max is an heir to a musical prodigy and an actor of the seventies and eighties, though he and his dad have a strange, even volatile relationship. He strived to be in the music industry like his father, Lou, but when Lou got into a drunken argument with his brother, Jack (Max's beloved uncle, who raised him), he removed Jack from his $2.9 million inheritance and kicked him out of the house Lou bought him, leaving Max with horrific detestation for his father and the music industry. I can tell it is bothersome that he hasn't yet exceeded his father's legacy, something only a handful of artists have done. This leaves Max with a lot of unresolved resentment, and hearing a song by his dad on the radio will spark a rage inside I have never seen as he will yell and change the station immediately, regardless of whether I like the song.

He is graduating in a few months from SMU with his master's in theater and English literature. He has that sultry look about him that English Lit majors have and stays true to his English roots by wearing a pea coat in the winter and loafers in the summer. With his thick, shiny blond hair and Chateau Marmot pool-blue eyes, he has the appearance of a well-maintained musician and adamantly plays his Les Paul every night. I am constantly on the fence regarding whether he is someone I should really be investing in. An English degree and well-bred hopes of making it in the music industry don't scream financial stability, or even a consistent work schedule.

"Hey, babe, what are you doing?"

"Nothing, just got back from that psychic I told you about. You?"

"Oh yeah, how'd it go? I just got off the phone with that little café spot where they want me to host an open mic night."

"Oh, no way! That's dope."

"Yeah, I mean, I'm not mad. I'd rather be performing, though. Like, 'NOW PUT YOUR HANDS TOGETHA FOR MIKE THE THUGH-EE-FIVE-YEAR-OLD

WITH FOU KEEDS AND FOUR MUMMIES WHO CAN'T UNDERSTAND THE INDUSTRY DOESN'T NEED HIM, YAY!'" Although I laugh, a small ache for him emerges, knowing he is jealous. I think about the text he sent me earlier:

> Hey, I called but no answer. I'm not sure where you are or if you're even planning on coming home. However, my opinion doesn't seem to matter to you, so here it is: Fuck you. How could you just leave without running this ridiculous idea by me? I guess we're not the "unit" like you've said? Good luck, I love you, but I'm moving out. Find someone else who's better at being dragged through the mud.

I pull the car over to the shoulder to study the text message again.

"What the FUCK, MOTHERFUCKER," I yell in shock. I realize it is kind of a spontaneous trip, but when you're looking for a critical diagnosis and have an idea who has it, you seek that person out.

"Selfish dick," I powerlessly say to the phone. He couldn't keep his anger under wraps for a few hours while I was out of service?

My eyeballs start to fill with liquid, and I feel that stupid ball in my throat and a pain in my gut. I check to see whether I have any bars so I can call him, explain myself, but nothing. No service.

I look around at my surroundings. Nothing at all except power lines in the distance, windmills, dehydrated and sparse patches of taupe grass and hunter-green foliage with dead tree branches and miscellaneous abandoned signs from the 1950s that say things like Jack's Toy Store. There are also dirt piles and vacant tractors appearing frozen in action. I look at my empty leather seat, imagining Max sitting there. I roll down the passenger window and hurl my iPhone at the clown sign.

I put my car in drive and get back on the empty highway heading west. I've written down my appointments on the backs of receipts, so I still have a hard copy of the doctors' information and appointment times. An hour later and missing my phone, I contemplate going back but don't have time. It is already 6:22 p.m., and I need to keep moving if I want to make it to El Paso by, say, midnight. I have an idea of inventing a GPS system that is in Snoop Dogg's voice.

"In approximately one thousand feet, my brotha, you gon' run up on this street called Whitaker and turn right on that bitch. Keep goin' down the road, ya hear me, and when you get to that stop sign, you gon' stop and turn luff on that Breeeeeeezy Street. Yeah cuhh, that is THE dumbass name of that street. Then OoOoooo-EEEE, there go your spot on the right after you gon' count to ten drivin' down that Breezy Street, cuz cousin, it's gon' turn into a new street name called Windhaven Road. Why they didn't keep it all one name, I don't have a damn clue. I ain't about no street-namin' life!"

Turn down the music. Now. Roll up the windows. Now. Stop eating. Now. Don't panic. It might go away. Hell no, it's here to stay. Deep breaths, God dammit. Hold on to the wheel, Poppy. Feel your feet. Try to keep your foot relaxed and distribute the same force that it has been at for the past thirty miles. Don't forget your foot. Don't let it float away. Make sure you hold it down. I fixate my eyes on the gas station sign ahead of me, next to a bus stop. No, don't worry. Keep driving. Don't let your foot off the gas, since you're not sure where the brake is or can't move your foot, and keep the wheel as steady as possible until this passes! And it will. Just keep breathing, driving, breathing and driving.

Chapter 4

Starfish

Starfish Motel, Colorado City, Texas

Tuesday, 9:29 p.m.

"Checking in?" asks a RuPaul look-alike. I know I have found the right place for the night with someone as interesting and glamorous as her working the front.

"Yes, well, sort of. Do you have a room for tonight?" I ask, gazing around at the art prints and the flashing Bud Light sign with a cord hanging down against a fuchsia backdrop.

"Yeah, we do have some vacancies. Gimme one…second," she says, inputting data on an outdated computer with three-inch-long acrylics, disguising her breasts (or lack thereof) in a baggy orange Hawaiian shirt, a hefty amount of makeup, and blinding Barbie-blond wig. "Your name?"

"Poppy Montgomery."

"Okay, hi, Poppy. I'm Ezzy, short for Esmeralda, if you need anything," she says, smiling but not looking up from her monitor. "Nice to meet you. How many nights?"

"Oh, just one."

"Any pets?"

"Nope."

"And are you expecting visitors?"

"Um…no. Actually, you know what? Maybe. I mean, who knows who I could meet at…where are we?"

"The Starfish Motel," she says with a lit-up stage smile.

"Right. Well, I can't predict the future. My boyfriend just broke up with me because I'm here with you instead of watching his band play, so I threw my phone out the window in Abilene."

"Oh, wow, child. It's a good thing there's a minibar in your room!" She winks and hands me a plastic card with a faded 103 scribbled on it with a Sharpie. "I've got you down in one-oh-three. Just go straight down the hall to your right."

"Sound good," I say, yawning and grabbing my stuff. "Hey, how much longer is the pool open?" I ask as I start down the hallway with peacock-feather carpeting.

"Until eleven, so you got about two more hours if you wanna swim. Are you a swimmer?"

I had never heard such a peculiar question from such a peculiar place and person. I, of all people, don't know how to respond.

"Well, I mean, I'm not a Michelle Phelps, but if a pool's there..."

Esmeralda smiles and nods, and I keep walking.

I plop down my suitcase on the eighties mint-and-peach floral bedspread that matches the drapes and smells like dead people. On top of the plastic-wood side table, a fat pink lamp sits with a cylinder canvas shade.

I find my flamingo bikini wrapped around my toiletries so they won't spill. I adjust my boobs in my top and eye myself in the full-length mirror, making sure everybody is tucked in and fastened before I head out.

"Well, hello," says Ezzy, sitting playfully by the pool with her feet in, not even five minutes after we met. She sports a solid-purple one-piece and a lime-green swim cap with white flowers. "Come for a dip?"

"Hello, again, and yes, I...suppose." I'm unsure what to think, since the woman working the front desk has migrated to the pool in record-breaking time.

"I would've guessed by now you would be making friends with the minibar in your room," she says softly, kicking her long, thin legs back and forth. I drop my towel and room key and kick off my flip-flops.

"Five years ago I would have dived right in, but not so much anymore."

"Really? Why five years?" she asks as I casually melt into the pool.

"That's how long I've been sober."

"Oh! No way. Congratulations. You, young lady, should be very proud of yourself."

When you get sober at a young age, people treat you as if you were a mermaid. Powerful and scarce, respected yet pitied.

"Thanks," I tell her and disappear underwater. Floating underwater feels like being in an alternate universe, or at least a world where I never have any attacks or episodes. "Are you off for the night?"

"No. I just like to come out here sometimes, look at the stars."

"Who's working the desk?"

"Well, I am, but I have a straight shot when I sit here to the front door, you see. Plus this is a slow time of night anyway," she says, dramatically lying back and getting a full view of the Texas night sky.

"I don't feel like I really did that much, though, y'know?" I say, trying to get the water out of my ear.

"To stay sober?"

"Yeah. That's all God's work. I mean, if it were up to me, I wouldn't be sober. I would be able to drink normally and still have a good life and enjoy myself and overdo it occasionally. Unfortunately, though, I have no interest in having one or two. Or three. It's an internal thing. I understand I'm powerless once it enters my body and it'll never be enough. Nothing will ever be good enough."

The ripples in the pool dance with our conversation.

"But you're so young! Honey, when I was your age, I was living in the Castro in San Francisco, trying to take over the world."

She picks up a bottle of Miller Light, and her glossy lips wrap tightly around the neck.

"You too? I went to college in San Francisco. How do you transition from San Francisco to this place? Where are we again?"

"Colorado City, child. The town of absolute nothingness. Save for some homophobes, ranchers, and racists." She throws back her beer into her mouth.

"Oh, but I bet you're their primary entertainment. They've probably never seen a transvestite before."

"Girl, I'd venture to say most haven't even seen a black person before. I'm just thankful I haven't gotten shot yet."

"So why are you living in this Podunk little town?"

"I don't know. I might move back to San Fran when I get my feet under me again. The owner asked me if I wanted to come out here and help him open a hotel since I have hotel-managing experience. It sounded wonderful and glamorous and sexy, thinking about opening my own hotel. He warned me it would be a smaller town, but I was ready for a change. Plus, I'm one in one million gays in San Francisco, and I'm one out of one gays in Colorado City. And I like the cowboys. I have a thing for the rodeo type. Like with that Matthew McConaughey accent. Girl, he can rope me in anytime he wants."

"Mm-hmm," I tell her, laughing, admiring her honesty.

"But whatchu doin' out here by yourself anyway? You ran away because your man left you?"

"Oh, no. I left him to come out here. Well, El Paso."

"Whatchu got goin' there?" She squints suspiciously.

"Well, long story short, I went to a psychic, and she told me that a diagnosis to a medical condition I've been suffering with would be there."

"Like what, if you don't mind me asking?"

"Oh no, you're fine. They're like these panic attack–like things or episodes. I get really anxious, then black out. It's the craziest thing. When I wake back up, I'm in a state of euphoria. It's weird."

"Oh, honey, I'm sorry. I get panic attacks too sometimes."

"Not like this. Well, maybe you do. But I feel like my brain's flipping inside out, and I say weird shit to people I don't know. Then I don't remember it. Then my organs and vagina feel like they're burning, and I get super nauseous."

"Lord, sounds terrible. You sure you not pregnant?"

I laugh at this awful thought. "No, ma'am."

"So you made doctor appointments in EP?"

"Yeah, I've got a few lined up so far," I say, yawning.

"Well, honey, good luck with that. I'll pray for you. Be careful though. You know how some doctors just throw prescriptions at you after talking to you for five minutes. My sister's been in and out of rehabs for heroin, but she initially got started on, like, Vicodin or OxyContin or OxiClean or something or other."

"Aww, I hate that for her. It happens all the time. At this point it's textbook. Doctor prescribes an opiate for a minor health issue. The patient gets hooked, goes broke, and switches to heroin."

"You're so right. And it's interesting because as a society, we overlook the housewife slurring her words because she's feeling the Valium she was prescribed because of her husband's affair, yet she somehow gets a pass because she's rich," Ezzy is saying, using her hands to get her point across. "Yet a broke prostitute with a shitty upbringing who does the same amount of Valium is clearly an addict because her hair's dirty or whatever."

I nod.

"My sister's now trying metha-or-something for her withdrawal."

"Oh, you mean methadone?"

"Yeah, that's it!" she says, sitting up straight and reaching for her beer.

"Oh, methadone. What a joke. Pharmaceutical companies will always be coming up with new things for people to get addicted to, to come off a previous addiction. Doesn't make sense."

"And the methadone or whatever is supposed to make you not have any withdrawal or something, right?"

"Yeah, then people get addicted to *that*. It's like, 'Here, take these, get addicted, then take something else after you realize you're screwed, and get addicted to that.' In my opinion, the addict needs to man up and just deal with withdrawal, not be tempted by some non-addict-brained prescriber who thinks replacing one drug for another mind-altering drug is the answer. I didn't have a pill or shot or patch to take for my withdrawals from Xanax and alcohol. I just powered miserably through alone in my apartment."

"Oh, wow. Yeah, the guy who owns this place had a problem with methadone or Suboxone too. Comin' in here all fucked up. Like, you have work to do and a hotel to run and people to feed, honey!"

"Pretty soon *everyone* will be walking around like zombies with no emotions or motivation other than getting more."

"I know that's right." She takes a drink. "Maybe the doctors want everyone high so they can conjure up some sort of scheme to…I dunno."

"You're probably right! Who knows what prescribers are really up to? What time is it?"

"It's eleven fifteen, so we're actually closed," she says, winking and standing up. I do the same, happy to have a meaningful conversation with someone but exhausted beyond belief.

"Wow, that's late. I need to turn in anyway. Good night, Esmeralda."

"Nice chatting, Poppy. I'll be praying, girl!"

"Thank you! Have a good night," I yell back and get my things.

Back in my room, I find a list of names, addresses, and appointment times for the next day with my Mapsco and fall asleep with it in my lap.

Chapter 5

Gas

An hour west of Midland, Texas

11:39 a.m.

Smells of dusky oil, sulfur, manure, and skunks occasionally seep through the windows. I can't get an attack with nothing to trigger them. No chaos, noise, flashing lights, or extreme temperatures. Only eerie land—dried and auburn, with bones of abandoned stores and homes time had its way with. Here there is no interest in real estate other than for drilling. It serves as a reminder of the mysteriousness and potential of uncharted land, before it is bombarded by concrete, men, and steel. I drive by a plethora of abandoned tractors, vintage signs, rusted cars, more lone houses, and gas stations, some in business, some out, and few to no humans in sight or other cars on the road.

Midland remains about an hour behind me when I stop at a Shell gas station around noon, excited to have human interaction. I fill up my car and ask the inside attendant in Spanish where the restroom is located, and she tells me outside, which is code for "We don't want customers in our indoor bathrooms, because they're disgusting and stricken with fatal diseases of all kinds." With the humidity on the rise, I roll my eyes at the thought of smelling an outdoor bathroom with shitty plumbing in Texas in May.

I jump when I open the heavy door and see a basset hound lying on the ground with droopy eyes and dried drool around its mouth.

"What the fuck? Hi, puppy," I say as I go to the bathroom, pretending it to be a normal sighting, and continue about my business, unsure of what normal is in what has to be the quietest town in the country. The flush roars and sucks with speed and noise to prove my preconceived notions wrong. I unlock the door and see the dog awkwardly watching me when the Dalmatian flashback occurs. I know what is coming.

When I get the attack, my perception of the world is shaken. I freeze, looking into the dog's eyes fearfully, suddenly insecure and unsure of the situation and whether I should tell someone there's a dog in the ladies' bathroom or I should run for my life. The insecurity I experience is handicapping. I try to mentally pull myself away, attempting to wash my hands. My senses are heightened, and I can smell the sulfur underground, the urine on the floor, and the fragrant floral hand soap from the shaky dispenser.

"Just breathe, Poppy," I say as I look into the mirror. No, don't look; it's too much. The rush comes again, more intensely. This time I shut my eyes because it's too frightening to leave them open and keep my balance. Everything turns into a tunnel that slowly turns black. My knees are bending.

"Dammit, go away," I (probably) say, with sensory overload climaxing. The dirty bathroom mirror with skinny pink graffiti, the dog, the heat, the cheap, sticky soap on my hands that smells like a garden exploded, the fact that my boyfriend is a jerk and I am traveling alone—all feel catastrophic. All the sensations and images compile in my mind in a kaleidoscope pattern. I put my hands on the sink and drop my head until it's over, trying to stay on my feet but powerless over my mind and body. I don't know what it is; I'll be forever stuck in an acid-trip-like life. Something is wrong with me, but I don't know what. My feet are burning. A heavyset Native American woman throws open the door and sees the dog and me with my head hanging. She jumps back.

"Hi, miss, are you okay?" she asks in a Spanish accent.

"Yes, I'm fine. I just need…do you have Valium or Xanax?" I unknowingly ask.

"No."

"Do you have water?"

"Let me go get you some!" She scurries off. I can hear her telling the clerk I am having some sort of meltdown and he should call an ambulance. I pull my heavy head up and try to stabilize myself when the euphoria comes, which is always last. Then I feel amazing, on top of the world. I start singing Elton John's "Benny and the Jets," dramatizing the "electric boots" lyric to what it actually sounds like "electric boobs."

The woman comes back with water, and I want to hug her. I feel as if I hadn't had water in days, hadn't seen her in years; she is like an old friend from when I was a kid whom I'd never met.

"I called ambulance for you. Are you okay?"

"Oh shit, no, call them back. I'm fine. I'm actually great!" I say, walking to hug her, reminding myself it is socially frowned upon to hug strangers, but I am elated to come back to my old self, to be where I think I am and I look as I used to. I remembered putting on my "I love Fridays like Kanye loves Kanye" shirt that morning. I see the bottle of Ozarka in my hand. I let out a sigh of disappointment. This means I probably humiliated myself and said something stupid and weird and told someone I needed water. It is a normal occurrence; I can't think too much of it. I reapply my lip balm and flip my hair to the other side, feeling refreshed and ready to get back on the road. I should be attack-free for a while since I just had one. It's scary but comforting once they're over; I feel as if I've just released a piece of anxiety that was weighing me down, because I know for the next hour (at least, I hope) or so, I'll be attack-free, not vulnerable and susceptible to the captivation of my mind, frightened of its capabilities.

I skip back to my car, forgoing gas. I peel out when I hear sirens a minute later and see an ambulance in my rearview mirror pulling into the station I just left.

By now I have the spells down to a science: I will get others around me involved because I want to tell someone what is happening as a defense mechanism, or just give someone the lowdown if I die from an attack. The EMTs come, see my blood sugar is low or normal, ask me my name and date of birth, whether I am in any pain, and whether I would I like to go to the ER. No and no are always my answers. The first time or two I blacked out, I went to the ER out of pure fear I was losing it. After I made full recoveries the same day and my parents got a couple of medical bills for $3,000 ambulance rides to the hospital to have the doctors tell me I was fine appeared to be wearing on them financially and myself mentally. I kept having the same problem but wasn't receiving any answers about what was really happening to me during those moments and why.

America's health care system seems to be driving people who need any sort of care away, for fear that surviving the heart attack or mammogram detection service means having to pay the outlandish $20,000-plus medical bills that throw people into bankruptcy every day, when in the end you may or may not win the medical battle that got you into financial ruin in the first place. If doctors are glorified drug dealers, then hospitals (in America) are glorified scammers.

Chapter 6

The Stones

120 miles away from El Paso

Wednesday, 10:37 a.m.

I feel strangely vulnerable and raw without my phone, like shopping without a bra or going to the Oscars with no makeup on. I am (I hope) on my way to Dr. Marks's office, the first one on the list. There are still few indications of civilization other than ranchers. How long will take for someone to find me if I have a heart attack? Radio stations are struggling to come through, and all I can get is mariachi music, which sounds like bright colors exploding and skirts twirling.

Drowning in boredom, I close my eyes for a few seconds, wondering how long I can drive with my eyes shut. Seven seconds is my longest. I roll up my windows only when I come across a manure, skunk, or sulfur smell; then they go right back down. It's eighty degrees and sunny. Suddenly, through the rattling maracas on the radio, I can hear, "I've been holding out so long, I've been sleeping all alone, Lord I miss you."

"Oh, hell yeah!" I yell as I turn up the radio and sing along with Mick Jagger. The Stones take me back to my childhood, when my dad would listen to them and Led Zeppelin constantly. My dad, Hugo, who comes from a musical family in New Orleans, naturally gravitated to wind instruments from observing street performers growing up. By the time he was twenty, he made a career out of playing backup for bands like the Who, Queen, Genesis, and Deep Purple.

Unfortunately, my dad couldn't keep blow out of his nose, which made band managers apprehensive to sign him. I remember he and my mom always getting into squabbles when I was young, when he did too much of what my mom called candy, and how could he when had a child at home? Before he met my mom, he spent time with other musician's girlfriends and borrowed their sports cars to drive around while he waited for his bandmates to sign autographs and give interviews. Along with stealing (borrowing) expensive cars, he would hook up with the girlfriends of the band members. One night postperformance he told one of the women he had a fling with that he was HIV positive, and she pulled a knife on him. He was rescued by the bus driver, who picked her up and pulled her off the bus, with one heel missing as she screamed and kicked in a rage, her permed hair covering her face, with blue eye shadow on her forehead. He eventually got sober in the mideighties, not long after he met my mom, Michelle, who gave him an ultimatum: get clean or get out.

Michelle worked the night shift as a nurse when one night when my dad came in for a toe he managed to break at four in the morning at a local diner. Said he had been up writing songs all night and got a craving for something sweet and since he had given up booze. On his way out, chocolate milk shake in tow, some asshole punk kid threw open the door, slamming it into his foot, removing his toenail and causing Hugo to make a loud noise and shout profanities. The drunken teen apologized and kept going, but Hugo went right to the hospital. "Men don't have much tolerance for pain," my mom always said.

In the middle of the "oo-whooOOOoooiiooo woo-ooOOO," it feels as if a volcano were about to erupt in my body. The nightmare continues. The monster is back. I wail in frustration.

Another one. Another outside force that temporarily possesses my brain, and no one knows what it is. I just want someone to tell me what is going on inside my head randomly for a few minutes I have no control over. This one, thankfully, isn't too intense. I keep quiet, intently focusing on the song so it doesn't overtake me. Maybe they're like rattlesnakes. If I don't fuck with them, they won't fuck with me. What are the odds that I won't get upset about them when they come? Come at me, motherfuckers. You won't reign over my mind and body and make me feel as if I'm going to lose control over my bladder and stomach. Who cares whether I pee myself? I'm a big girl; I can clean myself up. So what if you want to give me a heart attack or a stroke or make me lose consciousness? There are hospitals for those things.

Hopefully, I'll be able to remember my new plan of response to the next attack, but sometimes they romance me in a way that I succumb to them like a member of the Charles Manson family.

They are a part of my identity. I'm used to them; they're something familiar even though I hate them. Sort of like a woman who is dating someone who beats her because she was raised seeing her mother get abused, and even though she swore she would never go down that road, it's a familiar life for her, and most people would rather be in a shitty situation that is familiar than a safe situation they aren't used to.

I keep concentrating only on the road, keeping my hands and feet steady, able to maintain motor skills.

Sometimes I can predict their severity, but most of the time, they pull me in, grab ahold of me tightly by the throat, and I mentally trail off, captive on a sinking ship and heading for disaster. My family has told me I will yell out how much I hate these things and ask them whether they will they ever stop. If my mom is around, she tells me that I'm fine and to keep breathing. She says they're so frequent they don't concern her anymore.

I only want my brain to act as normal as everyone else's. Not in a boring way, but just to behave. Not make me feel and say weird, catastrophic things as if I were dying or the world were ending. I can't think about it too much, because it triggers them. The few days when I forget about them give me hope that they're gone for good, only to disappoint me in the next couple of days.

Stop thinking about it. Oh my God, Poppy! You just suckered yourself in! Here we go again; you've been ambushed! Powerless once again, here we go. I turn down the music and squeeze the wheel so hard my knuckles turn white. Hold on to the wheel. Feel your feet. Try to keep your foot relaxed, pressed firmly as it has been. Don't forget your hands. Don't let your foot float away.

This is bad.

I struggle to keep the wheel straight. The tunnel is deep; my feet are floating away from the pedals. I need to stop the car, but how? I can't access my motor skills to transfer my foot from gas to brake. Gravity is a thing of the past.

When I come back moments later, I am surrounded by strangers, a piercing siren, and blue lights. Right in front of me stands a giant Texaco pole, where my front bumper decided to kiss it passionately. I feel the euphoria but barely. I look around slowly in shock, trying to take it all in.

"Miss, are you okay?" I hear someone say. I look to my window at an older gentleman standing there, knocking on my window, trying to get me to roll down my window. I feel something wet on my hand and see a few drops of blood when I look down. I scan my body. My nose hurts. What happened? Why is there powder everywhere? Oh my God, the airbags went off. I'm alive.

My knee is hurting. I've had an attack and lost consciousness and have now wrecked my car. The sirens are getting louder. They are coming after me. I have gone too far this time. I will never be allowed to drive again. Wouldn't you know I'd be on my way to find a solution to the very thing that causes me to wreck my car, and now I have to go home? I'm done. I will forever be a woman with an uncontrollable, screwed-up brain that nobody has a fucking answer for, and it's ruining my life. I wipe the blood off my nose onto the deflated airbag and try to get some of the powder off my face.

"Miss, are you okay? Miss!" I unlock my door, partially in shock and partially afraid of moving if I'm injured. The EMTs open my door to see the damage and to question me.

"Oh my God," I yell again. It's more than I can handle. I am going to die.

"What…happened?" I ask, looking around hesitantly, afraid of what I might hear.

"I'm not sure, ma'am. You must have been distracted when you were driving. I was in my store reading the paper when I looked outside and saw your car slowly sliding off the road like this." He extends his arms forward and holds an imaginary wheel and slowly turns it off the road. He has a heavy southern accent.

"Oh, God. I'm sorry to scare you."

"No! Don't you worry about me. I'm more worried about you." Another paramedic, with his toolbox, slides in between us.

"Are you okay? Are you in pain? Does anything hurt?"

I slowly shake my head. "Well, my nose—it's bleeding," I say slowly, and he gets gauze from his kit.

"Well, you got some blood on you, and it looks like you might have spilled some coffee or something, because your shirt's all brown and wet. Would you mind just sitting down for me while I get your vitals?" I take the medic's arm, feeling weak, sitting down on the gravel like honey melting in tea. He takes my blood pressure, and two more paramedics arrive. These things now have the power to kill me, or someone else, completely sober. I'm losing it. Now I know how I'll die; it's no longer mysterious. I will eventually have an attack and drive off a bridge or a highway on accident.

"Okay, your blood pressure's a little high, but that's expected. Can you tilt your head back for me? I just wanna get a look at your nose. Airbag went off there."

He grabs tweezers from his toolbox.

"Does it hurt if I do this?" he asks, jiggling cartilage.

"Umm, no?"

"Okay," he says, putting his tweezers back. "Do you need to go to the hospital? I don't think your nose is broken, but you might wanna have it checked out just in case. Luckily, you weren't driving at too high of a speed when you tried to knock over this forty-foot pole. Were you on your phone or something? I don't smell alcohol on ya, and usually when there's a single-vehicle accident, alcohol or drugs are involved."

"Umm…yes, I was, and I shouldn't have…been on my phone. I was acting irresponsibly, and it won't happen again."

"Is she going to the hospital?" asks another paramedic, with a Caribbean accent.

"Nope, she's refusing,"

"Okay, I'll get the paperwork."

"Paperwork?" I ask, starting to feel the pain in my knee from it slamming into the dashboard. My chest is sore from the airbag.

"Yeah, since you're not going to the hospital, you need to sign a waiver. You sure you don't wanna go, just to be safe? I'd hate for you to be out here driving alone and something happen again. You on your way home?"

"Um, yes, actually."

"Okay, good. How far you got left?

"Um...I'm, like, twenty minutes out. Where do I sign?" I ask. The pole owner has his phone out and is taking pictures of the scene. This is just a baby accident, no big deal. I look around. Trees are swinging; the air is singing. The presumed pole owner is taking photos of me in a state of chaos with a gauze-stuffed nose as if I were a zoo animal.

"Hey, asshole, do you mind?" I ask. "I just got into a fucking car wreck, okay?"

He tells me he is doing it for insurance purposes.

Once I'm allowed to get up, I look at my Mercedes to see the damage of a sober, single-person auto accident; I'm looking forward to explaining the accident to insurance. I'll definitely need a new bumper, though it's only slightly dented but heavily scratched. I reverse, causing a minor shake due to the impact. For some reason car accidents sound and feel worse than they look, but at least I can drive it away.

"Stay off your phone, Poppy. Next time it could be worse," the all-American paramedic says before I drive away.

I'm soon back on the road with a ruined bumper and a clicking noise when I brake that didn't happen before the accident, but I drive on with my nerves shot but only fifty miles from my first appointment.

Chapter 7

Marks

El Paso, Texas

2:57 p.m.

"Hi, I have an appointment with Dr. Marks at three," I tell a thin woman with a worn face in orange scrubs sitting at a desk behind a glass screen dirtied with tiny fingerprints.

"Okay, and have you been here before or no?"

"No. New patient."

"Okay, and could you please fill out these forms for me? And I will let the doctor know you are here." She hands me a clipboard and pen.

"Yes, ma'am, will do."

"Do you have your insurance card with you?"

"No, I don't have insurance."

"Oh no! That's no good."

"Yeah, well, what can you do?"

I anxiously find a seat in the vacant waiting area. Under the windowsill the heavy sun is bleeding through blue blinds. The waiting room could use updating, but I'm not here for plastic surgery, so it serves its purpose. Scattered on the wall are framed images of deserts, horses, and cactuses. I pick up a *Texas Monthly* from across the room.

"Poppy?" I hear my name and roll my eyes thirty-five minutes later. Standing there is a Caucasian middle-aged man with a hunter-green cashmere sweater covering his potbelly. He has a full head of grayish-brown hair and wears thin, frameless glasses with an ID badge around his neck.

"Yes, hi." I stand up, wondering how his vacation was.

"Hi. Dr. Marks. Nice to meet you."

"Yeah, you too."

"My office is down here on the right, the second-to-last door."

I follow closely behind as he leads me out of the waiting room to his place of work.

"Right in here," he says, opening the door for me.

Inside are a black leather recliner and an emerald-green-and-white love seat, which faces his desk. He has a fishbowl on his table, like the kind you see in kids' rooms, with two gold and one purple fish, I forget the name, swimming around, looking confused, as fish do. His office smells like barbecue.

"Have a seat wherever you'd like."

"Okay, thanks." I choose the leather recliner and say a quick prayer when I set my bag down. On the wall hang his degrees from UT and Johns Hopkins.

"So what brings you in today?"

"Well, it's kind of a long story, but…I went to a psychic who told me that a doctor in El Paso would have a cure for my 'attacks' that I have. You were the first doctor to come up when I Googled doctors in El Paso, so…here I am!"

"Hmm, that's certainly interesting! Never heard that one before, but tell me about these attacks you have. Why do you put them in air quotes?"

"Oh, because I don't know what they are. I've had them since I was probably five or so, maybe even before. But I start off with this feeling like…I get a rush of anxiety from literally out of nowhere, for no reason. Sometimes when the lighting outside transitions from day to dusk and I can see it happening, then that triggers them, or if the weather changes. As a kid, when we'd have snow days, those were the worst. And holidays. I knew I'd have them all day long."

"And what were they like then, Poppy?" He takes notes.

"Well, like I said, it's a rush of anxiety I'm powerless over, and it feels like my brain is floating or sailing away, leaving me behind at the dock. Then it feels like my brain is literally doing flips and turning inside out. Then I'll get nauseous or afraid I'm going to lose control of my bladder. Sometimes there's, like, a black tunnel, and I'm drowning in it. A few minutes later, I snap out of it and get this rush of pure joy!" I study his face, hoping it shows signs that he understands what I'm talking about, like a doctor back in the day, when a patient would describe all her symptoms and he'd confidently nod his head, about to say, "You have a classic case of…" But Dr. Marks looks confused, as if I were telling him about people living on Pluto.

"It's bizarre because sometimes I feel like I can control them, maybe…I'm not sure. I hate them, but in a few moments, they're enticing, and I know at the end how good I'll feel, even if it's only for a few moments. Like I can't seem to say no, if I even have the ability to say no. I have no clue. I'm confused."

"Interesting. So have you ever peed yourself or thrown up during these spells?"

"Nope. I feel like I've had close calls though. Oh! I'll feel like I'm dying of thirst. When I lived in New York, I would ask people for water or a drink or weed or ecstasy, which is weird because I've never done ecstasy before, because it scares the hell out of me."

"But if you say you don't remember them, how do you know what you've said?"

"Oh! Because when I come back, I ask. Usually embarrassed and terrified about what could actually happen if someone roaming around Central Park actually gave me X or Valium. Oh, and they make super tired afterward."

"Uh-huh. So you're taking Zoloft now?"

"Yep." Wondering where he's going with the question.

"And that hasn't helped the attacks?"

"Not at all. Not sure why I'm on it, really."

"How long have you been on it?"

"I don't know. A *long* time. I would say I've been on it, like, twelve years?"

"Okay, well, I'm going to give you something to take when these attacks…you said you can feel them coming, right?"

"Yeah, most of the time."

"Okay, well, I'm going to give you something to take *only* when you feel these coming on, okay?"

"Okay, but what is it?" I ask, disappointed. I want a diagnosis, not a narcotic.

"The medicine or…"

"No! What do I have? What's wrong with me?"

"I'm not entirely sure. Some sort of severe panic episodes, though, it sounds like. But the medication I'd like to try is called Ativan, and it's in the benzodiazepine family, which can be addictive, so you need to use caution. Have you ever taken a benzo before?"

My face sinks, as I've heard this a dozen times prior. Some sort of anxiety seems to be the go-to when physicians don't know what's wrong with you. They say I have anxiety, and I ask them, who doesn't? Who in America doesn't have some sort of anxiety? I don't see them crashing cars, blacking out, and saying weird things to strangers while their brains go on an underwater roller coaster and their eyes twitch and they mentally break from conversations and situations without wanting to.

"Hell yeah. In college, when I was drinking all of the time to help my hangovers."

"Oh, no. It's serious if you drink. Do you still drink? I thought I saw on your chart that you…" He digs through his paperwork in his lap.

"Nope, six years sober."

"Congratulations, that's a very difficult thing to do. You should be proud of yourself."

"I was at first. Then I realized I have nothing to do with it, so…the glory here goes to God."

"Very good, Poppy. Do you remember how well how it worked or didn't work for you with these spells?"

"Um, negatively, I think. I really don't remember. I still had them, but not as frequently, I think."

"Does anyone in your family have anything like your attacks?"

"Not like I do," I say, disappointed. *Nobody* has anything like I do. And I've asked around.

"Okay, well, let's try the Ativan. Remember to only take it as needed, okay?" I nod. Maybe I can handle benzos now, since I really have a serious issue, and not take them because it's tax season or the sky is the wrong shade of blue.

"All right, then. Alex will check you out at the front." I picked up my Gucci bag and exit, unfulfilled, though slightly hopeful.

"Hi, Poppy, okay. So Dr. Marks would like to see you back in two weeks, so that puts us at the middle of May. Do you prefer mornings or afternoons?"

"Um, I live in Dallas, so getting back may be an issue." I have no interest in ever seeing the doctor again. "Actually, I think I'll be back around then for work," I tell her.

"Okay, so how does eight thirty sound?"

"Wonderful," I say, smiling.

"Perfect, let me put you in the system. And today your out-of-pocket is two hundred fifty dollars."

I hand over my debit card as I watch my life savings get swiped away from me.

Chapter 8

El Paso

Holiday Inn Express, El Paso

5:08 p.m.

Finding a hotel in El Paso, in comparison to Colorado City, is a breeze. The Holiday Inn Express will be my home for the night. I grab my suitcase and stand behind a couple in line wearing matching Hawaiian shirts. The lobby smells like chlorine sanitizer mixed with fresh laundry, not like pickles and dead people like at the Starfish Motel. I'm hungry, it's almost noon, and I need to go pick up my Ativan from the Walgreens.

A millennial European couple walks in, making me wonder about Max and whether he's tried to reach me at all. I decide they're European because of how often they look up and point; plus the light eyes and hair with Polish specialty luggage are a dead giveaway. These are just some of the many things I observe since I'm not glued to my phone: things called humans and life.

"Hi, may I help you?" asks a two-hundred-pound raven-haired Latina with crusty lipstick.

"Yeah, I just need a room for tonight. For one."

"Did you reserve a room or no?"

"Nope."

"Okay, let me see what vacancies we have. Give me one second."

"Sure."

I glance back at the people in line. Americans on business trips are scattered in the lobby, enjoying margaritas and beers. She hands me a key card. I'm going to be on the eleventh floor. I get to my room and look out the window to see whether I have a view of El Paso, the city with my supposed diagnosis for my chronic, mysterious condition.

Red mountains and plateaus are scattered in the distance, along with tall buildings but not skyscrapers, and the sky is clear. Somewhere out there is a doctor waiting for me to find him or her so he or she can fix me. There's a couple at the pool below, basking in the coating sun with drinks next to their lounge chairs. My stomach growling is my cue I need to pick up my medicine and eat. I ask for directions to a Walgreens from a bellman out front.

He recommends a popular eatery called E & J's café. I decide to give it a shot since he says it's the best in town. I swing into the Walgreens parking lot, suddenly anxious about getting the sister drug to what almost killed me four years ago. I pay seventy-five dollars for my addictive controlled substance prescribed by someone who is aware I have an addiction problem.

I look at the package, and it glares back at me from the passenger seat, waiting to be ripped open, reminding me of my dark past obsessions. Dr. Marks said to take them only "as needed," but as someone in recovery, I'm not very good at the "as needed" judgment call. I tell myself it is different from Xanax and I shouldn't be fearful of another addictive substance because I've had a shady past. I will wait to take one, try the "as needed" thing like a normal person. I listen to El Paso's finest radio stations and cruise to E & J's. The AS NEEDED ONLY phrase glows in my mind like lights on Broadway. As needed. Only take it if you *need* it, so it's as needed. What the fuck does that even mean? I ask the benzodiazepine gods below.

E & J's café

5:30 p.m.

Dark, romantic lighting and black vinyl booths (some torn with orange stuffing coming through) set E & J's ambiance. All kinds of goofy photos of people who've eaten there hang on the wall. The slot machines and extensive beer collection create a vibe of small-town camaraderie.

I choose the Mexican sampler for dinner and am not disappointed. It's the most authentic Mexican cuisine I've had in a while, the last time being in Dallas at a place called Manny's, where Max got into a bar fight about a "sports disagreement" and we were asked to leave.

I eavesdrop on the conversation the couple in the booth behind mine is having. From what I gather, they aren't from Texas. They are talking about a cemetery close by a couple of centuries old that's home to famous, deceased Texas outlaws.

I sip my iced tea and listen to the couple talk about a hippie commune where everyone hangs out and shoots heroin all day. I imagine the lunacy of such a place. Some people can be so naïve. Perhaps they are talking about a dream or a movie, and I missed that part.

I go for a walk to the Concordia Cemetery, the sky marked only with airplane exhaust. What looks like hundreds of crosses decorate the massive cemetery, all aligned a couple of feet apart in an orderly, clean stance, almost contemporary, on grassless land. The silence is haunting; you can hear only the wind. No birds are chirping, and no one is visiting.

Holiday Inn Express, El Paso

7:10 p.m.

After a useless diagnosis, a popular eatery, a strange cemetery, and thirty days of Ativan judging me, I'm ready for a good night's sleep. I debate calling my parents but assume they'll probably think I'm fine and with Max somewhere. I flick on the old-school television set after I wash my face. I hear people at the pool and get up to see who is there and how El Paso lights up at night, when I hear a news anchor: "Twenty-five-year-old Poppy Montgomery was last seen by her parents on Saturday afternoon, her hair in what her mom calls a messy bun. If you or anyone you know has seen this young woman, you are urged to call the Dallas police department immediately." There's a huge photo of me on the television set with the word "MISSING" underneath it.

"Oh my God! Shit! Here I am! They filed a missing person's report?" I rush downstairs to the lobby, wondering why my parents didn't use a better photo of me to show to the world.

"Can I borrow your phone? It's an emergency," I tell the concierge. I'm not sure whether people are looking at me because I'm panicked or because they just saw me on TV. The phone is picked up after two rings.

"Mom! It's me! Why would you file a missing person's report?"

"Oh my God, Poppy! Hugo, your daughter's on the phone! Where the hell are you? Are you okay? We're out looking for you everywhere! Max hasn't heard from you other than you telling him you've left for El Paso!" She is hyperventilating.

I explain the situation, trying to calm her down. She proceeds to tell me how irresponsible it is and how selfish I am to have them worry like that, blah, blah, blah. I explain that having a phone is holding down my full potential and I don't like being addicted to a toy. She rants and rages as moms do about "missing people" when they're not actually missing. I feel like a teenager again, and she tells me to stop acting like one and I need to come home. Instead I head to the pool.

I much enjoy watching people's drinking behaviors when I'm at a bar or restaurant. It's amazing how slow normal drinkers drink. Alcoholics drink faster than average. In fact, a lot of times, it's best to order two drinks at a time because the waiter may die and you could have to wait for drink number two. There's an old method to tell who's an alcoholic when they're out at a bar and there's a fire. Alcoholics will take (or finish) their drinks before evacuating; normals leave theirs to burn, not thinking twice. I jump in the pool, ready for a second wind and to psychoanalyze the couple drinking with matching Hawaiian shirts. I float underwater, trying to stay down. I can hear them from the bottom of the pool.

"Hey!" I hear him yell. I roll my eyes underwater.

"Yeah?" I ask, coming up.

"I just wanted to make sure you could breathe! Wait, haven't I seen you before?" he asks.

"Yeah, probably here," I tell him.

"No, I mean…doesn't she look like that girl on the news we just saw, Annie?" He nudges Annie as she digs in her purse for something, her cleavage spilling out. Annie stops and glares at me.

"Yeah, kinda. But her hair's wet, Rob. It's hard to tell!"

"No shit, Annie. I mean, DUH, her hair is wet! But you…she…you're not missing, though, right?" he asks, confused.

"Nope! That couldn't be me. You must be thinking of someone else." Intoxicated people are the easiest to fool.

"Yeah, Rob, we just saw her from the lobby," says Annie, probably in her midthirties with dark hair and eyes and pale skin. "What's your name?" she asks.

"My name is…Jessica. You?"

"I'm…my name is Annie, and this is Rob," she says, pointing. He awkwardly waves, adjusting his glasses.

"Nice to meet you. Where are y'all from?" I ask, putting my elbows on the edge of the pool.

"New Orleans. You?"

"Dallas. Nola? Nice. I love it there. Lots to do, see, and drink," I say with a smile.

"Yeah, we like it. Rob here, my husband, is from Florida."

"Cool. What brings y'all out here?"

"A funeral." Annie goes into a long stretch of details about her cousin who tragically died in car accident by a drunk driver, and she's decided to drink away her grief while in El Paso. I appreciate the honesty. I would be drinking myself away and wouldn't know why. Rob butts in the conversation, telling Annie she and her cousin weren't that close, followed by a brief argument about Annie and her cousin's volatile relationship.

"What about you? Why are you here?" Annie asks, simultaneously telling Rob she wants a Crown on the rocks.

He flashes me a half smile and gets up, kissing her on his way in. Annie and I chat about New Orleans, college, and my sobriety. Rob comes back with a drink, and I get out of the pool. She takes a gulp of her Crown. Annie went to Arizona State for college and studied marketing, and she and Rob have been married for almost a year.

She says the Hawaiian shirt was a dare from one of their friends, and if they asked ten nonnative English speakers where Hawaii was and filmed it, their friend would give both Annie and Rob $500 in cash. She shows me the footage of confused locals as they struggle to tell them in English how far away Hawaii is and how they could be so stupid, when they are clearly in El Paso, saying things like, "You are stupid, man. Do you see the beach? No! Mountains here, only! You see cactus, mountains, dry weather. No beach, no." We all three laugh, mimicking his hand gestures as he points to the mountains and rocks. Annie and Rob are turning out to be quite entertaining.

Again, out of nowhere, it hits like a brick wall. I want to crawl into a powerless, weak hole and die. Strike one for Dr. Marks. The Ativan won't suffice as a preventative measure against these mental monsters. I try to stay calm midconversation, not zone out or stare anywhere for too long. I assume since Rob and Annie are liquored up, they won't notice my brief mental instability. This one seems to last longer than normal, but before I ask for drugs or anything, Rob beats me to it.

"What do y'all say you come up to our room and we'll keep the party goin'? These kids are…annoying," Rob says, motioning toward the child guests who have arrived without a chaperone and who also like to swim, laugh, and yell. Little do they know my brain is also going for a swim. I am dizzy, confused, and disoriented but per usual have no inhibitions about anything. I have no control, no rationalization ability. I just say whatever will get my mind off the monster the quickest so (maybe) it will go away.

"Yes, please," I tell them, standing up. The last thing I need (or want) is some drunk weirdos trying to kill me or do some voodoo séance in a hotel room. My legs are burning. Stop it, stop it, this will be fun. Go away, you piece of shit. Maybe a change of scenery will help, and if I push it enough. Just don't say anything, Poppy, or try not to. The pool though. I've been here before, haven't I? I study the green pattern on the carpet, smelling its scent of dried rubber, laundry detergent, and perfume. I can't recall what Annie and Rob are saying. I'm silent, trying to put together where I've seen and smelled the carpet before. It must have been when I was in daycare.

When we reach Annie and Rob's room, he throws open the door proudly, and when I step in, there's an array of handcuffs, feathers, whips, packages of anal beads, blindfolds, and lingerie all over the place.

"You want a drink?" Rob asks.

"Um…yes?" I say, slowly.

"Are you okay?" Annie asks.

"No, I mean, no drink. I don't drink," I manage.

Rob quietly closes the door and approaches me from behind, startling me and sending a chill up my spine.

"How do you like it, Poppy?" he asks. His voice has to have lowered ten different octaves; he says it as though in slow motion. I start to feel it. The spell is ending. The euphoria is coming.

"Um, however you want it," I say, trying to humor him, still unsure of the situation I'm in. He slides his fingers down my back. Annie starts to undress and lies on the bed, watching Rob and me. Annie gets up and pushes my bikini strap off my shoulder, smiling while I'm buzzing with euphoria. Rob goes down on Annie. I finally come back to normal.

Oh my God, where are you? These people are swingers, Poppy! I must have followed these strangers into their room in an attack.

"He asked you how you wanted it," says Annie, struggling to get the words out. I'm disgusted with myself, terrified how I'll get out of this mess.

"Oh shit! Hold on, I forgot my phone. Let me go get my phone. I'll be right back," I tell them and dart out, hoping they don't chase after me with weapons. I hear Annie yell that I didn't have my phone with me. I run back into my room, mortified, and double-bolt the door. Though it is too late, maybe an Ativan will help. I hop in the shower to get the chlorine out of my hair, along with any of Rob's and Annie's DNA.

Chapter 9

Wells

Holiday Inn Express

Thursday, 7:05 a.m.

I wake up at five and immediately check out, forgoing my free breakfast to avoid any awkward run-ins with Rob and Annie. I am on my way to meet Dr. Wells, located a bit on the outskirts of town. I have an hour until I need to be there, and decide to cruise around, passing by a gas station that has burned down or disintegrated over time, leaving only the remains of the fueling area, like a trailer park version of ancient ruins in Rome. I have a million questions about the residents who once vacated or owned these shops. Where are they? Why did they leave? Were they forced out? It appears that way. West Texas is like an antique dollhouse that's worn and tattered since the owner abandoned it two hundred years ago.

Dr. Wells's office

8:30 a.m.

"Hi, I have an appointment with Dr. Wells," I tell a brunet receptionist in hunter-green scrubs. She has single-length, mousy gray-brown hair and chalky skin covered in foundation that isn't the right shade, though she probably doesn't know it.

"Poppy?"

"Yep!"

"Okay, if you want to have a seat and fill out this paperwork, he'll be with you shortly."

"Okay, great."

"Oh, Poppy, did you have your insurance card with you?"

"Nope."

"Okay, so…you'll be paying out of pocket?"

"Yes, that's correct."

"Okay, well, just have a seat, and the doctor will see you soon."

I sit next to a fish tank and try to fill out the redundant questionnaire with all the fish spying on me. I watch them go back and forth, look at me, their scales shimmering in the light, spit something, poop, turn around, and swim the other direction.

"Poppy?" asks a tall man in his late thirties who resembles a young Fidel Castro.

"Yep!"

"Hi, I'm Dr. Wells. Nice to meet you."

"You as well."

Inside Wells's office are a few succulents and a desk, a computer, and a brown suede sofa with pillows begging to be beaten. I sit down and observe him as he observes me.

"So tell me about yourself, Poppy," he says with his hands clenched in a fist on his desk. I want to tell him I like traveling and yachts and kittens and chocolate and anything lavender but figure that wasn't what he meant.

"Well, gosh, where to start? Okay, I went to Stonewall High School in Stonewall, Texas, went to art school in San Francisco, lived in New York, where I was abused as a fashion intern, then moved to Portland to be with a boyfriend and wasn't crazy about the weather, lack of jobs, and how all of the people looked the same. So I'm back in Texas."

"What do you mean, you were abused as a fashion intern?"

"Hmm." I smile. "I was fresh out of college with no clue what to do with my life, so I interned for companies like Rouge and independent stylists. They didn't like me, so I got fired for working for free. Did you know, Dr. Wells, that you could get fired working for free? In 2010, when the economy was absolute shit?" He smiles, trying to gauge my sanity. It's always fun to confuse doctors, since neither of us really knows what is going to come out of my mouth. I know I'm not crazy, so I just let things roll off the tongue.

"Well, I'd imagine, if you didn't perform to their standards. What'd you get fired for?"

"Which time?"

"Start with the first."

"Oh, Ladies Wear It. I might have PTSD from working at that sweatshop. They were paying me, like, ten dollars a day to live in New York and run these errands and be dismissed by all the higher-ups who thought they were the shit, not to mention the other clown interns I had to work with, like, 'Oh, you're so pretty, I love your shirt, you want me to do what? Go get you Cheetos and monogrammed highlighters while you stick your Gucci-flavored dildo in my—'" I stop before he has me committed.

"That bad, huh?" he asks, scratching his beard and crossing his arms so they rest comfortably on his belly.

"Yeah. I can't deal with fashion people in New York. You're not original, girl. Who cares who you wear? Go find a meaningful existence not bombarded with who wore what and diets and call sheets." I feel relief wash over me, sharing all my pointless information about my time in New York.

"Well, what did you take away from those experiences?" I'm disappointed Wells doesn't chime in with any gossip or feedback.

"Well, not to ever live in New York since everyone moves too fast, it's overpriced, more commercial than creative, and people who hire interns are scam artists."

"Okay, so you learned something, though."

"Yeah, more than I wanted to."

"But why don't you tell me what's really bothering you. What brings you here today?"

"Um...I went to see a psychic who told me to go to El Paso and see a doctor because I have these panic attacks or episodes where I go unconscious and it feels like my brain is being taken over...and then it comes back, and all is well."

"Are the episodes telling you to do things, or are you hearing any voices during these episodes?"

"Nope! Just my normal self."

"Mm-hmm, and how long have you had these?"

"Forever, all my life. No one has been able to help me, so that's why I'm here. I wrecked my car on my way here from Dallas. I need answers."

"Oh no, are you okay? I'm assuming."

"Yeah, just trying to solve this dilemma so I don't drive off a bridge or hit a child crossing the street during a blackout."

Dr. Wells goes on to ask me more about my medical history, overall health, medications, eating habits, and family history, while he configures a response in his head.

"Okay, I think I may know what it is."

"WHAT!"

"A gluten allergy." A long pause comes, and I roll my eyes.

"Shut up, are you serious? You're telling me gluten can cause what goes on in my head and causes me to wreck my car and mentally check out without my permission?"

"I'm saying there's a possibility, Poppy. At least it's a good start to get you feeling better."

"But I feel fine, though. Not sick, just mental."

He goes on to explain how crucial a healthy, balanced diet is to our overall health and how gluten allergies can cause a lot of mental health problems. Could he be right? Could I really be dealing with a food allergy? The more I think about it, the dumber I feel, and I am going to have to pay big money for this diagnosis.

Chapter 10

Connelly and Bourke

El Paso, Texas

Thursday, 11:14 a.m.

I get some coffee, say a quick prayer, and step into the doctor's office. I get the same greeting as at the other doctors' and a similar setup, with chairs and coffee tables with outdated magazines thrown around on top.

"Poppy?" a tall, Nigerian man asks, half an hour later.

"That's me."

"Yes, hi, nice to meet you. My name is Dr. Connelly." His strong Caribbean accent makes me remember the cruises my family used to take to Belize and Jamaica. "So how can I help you?" he asks, motioning for me to sit wherever.

"Long story short, I need an answer to these spells I have, and a psychic told me to come to El Paso, so hopefully the doctor is you." His pearly white teeth shine when he smiles.

"Well, okay then! Hopefully I can be of assistance to you. First of all, what are your spells, you say? What happens to you?"

"First I feel anxious, then I feel, like, a wave come over my body and like my brain is flipping inside out. I say and do things I normally wouldn't had I not had—"

"Like what?"

"Um, well, last night I was invited to go to this couple's hotel suite, and I actually said yes because I was in the middle of an attack. I think I use people as a defense mechanism maybe. It's kind of my brain's way of distracting itself from what's going on by getting other people involved. Usually I'll ask for drugs or a drink, even though I don't do either anymore."

"Oh my goodness, Poppy! Yeah, I've looked, and your paperwork says you've been sober for a while, yes?" I nod. "So I'm wondering why you would be doing these crazy things if you're sober."

"That's a million-dollar question. I also tell people my feet are burning and I need water and that I can't breathe. At least that's what other people have said who are around to witness, but I have no recollection of saying or doing them."

He asks other questions about my medication history, family history, and so on.

"Have you ever had a brain scan or what's called an EEG?"

"Nope."

"Okay, you know what then? I'm going to order one. That way I can get an idea of your brain activity, and if there's been any trauma or if something isn't working as it should, the scan should be able to tell us that." Though it isn't a diagnosis, I'm happy he offered a different troubleshooting solution and didn't immediately want me taking any narcotics. I leave hopeful, even with a $175 bill, but Dr. Connelly is cheaper than the other two and offered something unique that could lead me to the answer I am seeking. Although I don't plan on coming back to his office, I can take his recommendation to other doctors in Dallas, but when a brain scan or any other medical machinery is used, without insurance I need to expect to pay around $10,000 for a fancy x-ray.

El Paso, Texas

Thursday, 2:05 p.m.

Immediately following my appointment with Dr. Connelly, I am meeting with Dr. Bourke, who is conveniently located about three miles away.

"Hi, I have an appointment with Dr. Bourke." This time an Asian woman hands me a clipboard with obvious paperwork to fill out and sign and date, fill out and sign and date, repeat. Same questions over and over again about my mood, medications, surgeries, medical and family history, and so on. Same chairs, though this office doesn't have a television or fish tank, and it smells like vanilla sugar cookies.

"Poppy?" I hear a quick five minutes later.

"Yes, hi," I say, eyeing the older, tall gentleman with slightly crooked teeth and a lean physique.

"First we need to get your vitals, and Karen will do that. Then I'll meet you in my office in a few minutes, okay?"

"Okay, thanks!"

Karen gets my weight—an alarming 126—asks me what pills I've taken today and last night and whether I recreationally use drugs or drink, and finally gets my blood pressure before she sends me on my way to the third door on the left.

"Come in," Bourke says in a baritone voice. "Just have a seat wherever. And tell me, what brings you in today?"

I tell him the story, fleshing out details as they come about my attacks and eyeing his framed credentials. Harvard Medical. I have a good feeling about him. He should definitely know what's up, with a prestigious undergrad and med-school education.

"Yeah, and so far I've just gotten benzos, one guy told me it was a gluten problem, and one ordered an EKG or whatever." He pushes up his glasses.

"Hmm, don't you have a problem with addictions? Why would someone prescribe you Ativan?"

"Beats me. Probably so I get addicted and have to keep coming back."

"How's your sleep, Poppy? How much do you regularly get a night?"

"Um, during the school year, probably five to nine hours. It depends."

"You're a student?"

"No, a teacher."

"Oh, very good. What grade?"

"All of them. I teach art, pre-K through fifth."

"Ahhh," he says, smiling and tilting his head back. I've noticed a lot of people with this reaction, as if suddenly I make more sense to them or it must be a humbling, rewarding, and morally satisfying job, which it is, but I could never do it if I weren't sober. I don't understand how more teachers don't drink on the job, especially with younger kids. You could probably get away with it since they wouldn't know, and I'm sure the teacher would be much more fun to the students. Too bad the teachers I've explained this theory to aren't interested in drinking on the job. Before I got sober, that's how I survived through work!

"Wow, you're doing the Lord's work, you know it?"

"Yep, seems that way. But I love it—most of the time. When the kids are behaving as they should and they really enjoy an assignment. Luckily, though, I haven't had an attack while teaching. It seems when my brain is a hundred percent occupied in the moment, I don't really get them. It's usually when my brain has some free time and space and doesn't need to be hyperfocused. That's when it's bad: driving, being in a car, on an airplane. Bikram yoga is a big one too, with the heat."

"Oh, you do yoga? Regularly?"

"Yeah, pretty much. But the heat usually triggers an attack, so I have to really be on guard."

"I see. Do you feel like you can prevent them?"

"I dunno. It feels like I can for, like, ten quick seconds maybe—if I did a headstand really quick, it wouldn't catch me. It's like being possessed by the devil, because I try and stay away, but when I give it a second thought, it catches me in its terrifying grip."

"And you can't stop them?"

"No, I don't think. Not once I'm in. It seems like the world stops once I'm in my mental galaxy, and I have no control."

He takes notes. Clouds are accumulating outside.

"So what do you think?" I ask, wiggling my toes in anticipation.

"Well, I unfortunately think we're out of time for today, but I'd like to investigate this further. Have you ever done any cognitive behavioral therapy?"

I can feel gravity pull down my face. He thinks I need therapy for this? "No. Well, yes, in rehab. Have you? Are you in therapy?"

"That's not something you should ask your health care provider," he says, smiling. He obviously doesn't know what's wrong. If he thinks this is something therapy alone can fix, he needs a new career.

Chapter 11

Wang

El Paso, Texas

Thursday, 2:56 p.m.

The brick building that houses my next doctor's office is squatty and most likely built in the 1950s. A few more cars in the parking lot than the last place. I say a prayer and walk inside.

"Hi, I have a three o'clock."

"Hello, are you…Poppy?"

"Yes, ma'am!"

She hands me the usual and asks about money. "Just bring those back when you're done, and Dr. Wang will be with you shortly."

"Okay, thanks." I sit down in one of the dining room chairs in the waiting area to fill out my paperwork while listening to the local news that's playing on the eighties television above my head. I look up, wondering how much a settlement payout would be if it fell on someone's head and he or she survived. I answer the survey questions about my mood.

1.   On a scale of 1–10, how would you rate your level of anger today? 7.5.

2.   True or False: I often feel that everyone I love is dead. False.

3.   On a scale of 1–10 with 10 being the highest on the agree scale, how much do you agree or disagree with the following: I often feel as though I'm worthless, that the world would be better off without me. Shit no. 0.

"Poppy Montgomery?" asks an Asian woman in a white doctor's coat. "Hi, I'm Hayley, Dr. Wang's nurse. Nice to meet you."

"You, too."

"We need to get your weight real quick." I roll my eyes, thinking of my Mexican heaven I consumed earlier.

"Okay, one twenty-six," she says, writing on a file. I make my best "Well, that's what happens" face to myself, not because I am actually upset but that's just what I think women are supposed to do when they get weighed. Plus I've been sitting in a car for over twenty-four hours, which burns about negative eighty calories an hour. Whatever. I'm technically on vacation, so there's no calorie counting. I'll buckle down and eat greener when I get back to Dallas.

From the degrees and photos hanging, I learn Dr. Wang is an internal medicine doctor, not a psychiatrist. However, Wanda didn't specify *which* type of doctor would know my diagnosis.

I hop on the table covered in taut white tissue paper, which crumples and sounds as if a baby elephant sat down. A few minutes pass. No sign of Wang, no phone to occupy my time. I meditate, struggling to clear my mind, and wonder whether I'm actually meditating if I'm thinking about meditating and how I should feel if I am, perhaps, meditating. Someone knocks before I can decided whether meditating means no thinking or thinking about not thinking.

"Come in." I sit up to appear normal.

"Poppy? Hi, I'm Dr. Wang." She extends her hand. I'm surprised that she is a woman, since I obviously have an outdated, sexist bias against female doctors. She wears a white monogrammed coat with a stethoscope around her neck.

"Hi, I'm Poppy."

Doctors always introduce themselves and ask the general "How can I help you?" which sounds like drug-dealer lingo, or "What brings you in to see me?" which also sounds drug dealer–esque. But they hand out scripts for oxycodone, Roxicodone, Percocet, Demerol, Xanax, Klonopin, Adderall, fentanyl, Vicodin, morphine, and Valium, which are precursors to street drugs, so physicians are more similar to the bad influences you don't want your kids around than is the dope fiend who's lost nearly all and is homeless.

I tell Wang my story, for what feels the millionth time, about the psychic and being from Dallas and how I'm searching for a cure.

"Well, that's interesting! Well, maybe I'll be able to help you. Can you tell me what's going on?" she asks, getting her pen ready to strike.

"Yeah, I've been told they're a form of panic attacks, but basically I experience a floating sensation, my feet will burn, and I'll tell someone to take my shoes off or that I need water or ask strangers if they have Xanax or decide to go into strangers' bedrooms who turn out to be swingers, just to name a few. But I don't remember saying these things. Usually when I snap out of it, someone will be there and tell me what I said. I'll usually, by then, be exhausted or get really bad headaches. Does this sound like something you've heard before?" I ask impatiently.

"Oh, so you were already given a diagnosis of panic attacks?"

"Yep."

"Because usually when people have panic attacks, they also feel powerless over them and wish they could forget them but can't. So to me that's peculiar." I smile at the promise of her observation.

"Well, what else could it be?"

"Um, it's actually tough to tell. You said you've had these your whole life?"

"Yep, since I can remember, like, since I was five."

"Okay, and have you had any head injuries in your life? Like, let's see, have you been in any car accidents or anything else that caused trauma to your head?"

"I've been in car accidents but nothing major where my head was hit directly."

"Okay, what about sports? Baseball, basketball, anything like that?"

"You mean have I been hit in the head with a soccer ball? I did gymnastics."

"Well, a lot of times sports injuries don't show up right away. I mean, when we look at the concussion rate of pro football players, sometimes they don't have any issues until years and years later."

"One time when I was four, I fell and hit my head on a coffee table."

She looks perplexed. "And when your head hurts after these attacks, where is the pain?"

I point to my temple and base of my head. "Here and here."

"How long does your pain last?"

"Um, about half an hour."

"Have you ever been diagnosed as bipolar or placed on bipolar meds?"

"Nope!" I say, knowing that whatever I have is not bipolar disorder. These are short but more frequent episodes where I lose control of my speech and my body.

"Okay, well, I want to start you on something called Lamictal, which is a bipolar medicine. I need to get further info on you to determine if you are bipolar, but it seems like when you describe the highs and lows of the episodes, it, to me, sounds very similar to someone who is bipolar."

"But I don't go on spending sprees or try to go to the moon or blow up and throw things and yell at people or post a thousand things on social media a day."

"Well, Poppy, we have different variations of bipolarity, and some people experience some symptoms, and others experience other symptoms. It's all a manageable disorder when patients take their meds, but…" she says, writing. "I'm also going to give you something for the pain you describe, called hydrocodone."

I roll my eyes at her carelessness. She just wants me to keep coming back.

"Have you ever had major surgeries?"

"Yeah, I've had my wisdom teeth removed."

"Okay, so I'm sure your dentist had you on some pain meds. I think a tiny dose after you have your episodes will calm your nerves and lessen the tension in your head, which *may* prevent future attacks. Sounds like your brain is experiencing some form of PTSD."

"Yeah, well, I'm not, to my knowledge."

She says she wants to see me in no more than three weeks, since I'm starting on a new med, but I've lost all respect for her and wouldn't come back even if I could. If anything is necessary for pain after a spell, it's a couple of Advil, not hydrocodone. She tells me not to crush or snort it, saying that intensifies the effect. A doctor telling that to a patient is like telling teenagers they can't drink alcohol until they're twenty-one. What are the odds that maybe, just maybe, I *am* bipolar? This could be it.

"Okay, so today your visit is two hundred fifteen. How would you like to pay?"

Luckily, this is my last appointment for now. I need to check my savings to see how much longer I can afford to get fraudulent, bullshit diagnoses.

"Card."

Chapter 12

Orlando

After five doctors and still having attacks, I've had enough. I'm angered about the couple of thousand dollars I've thrown away to receive false diagnoses from clueless physicians. This appears to be a waste of time and resources. I'm done. I was in a single-vehicle accident, almost became a snack for a set of swingers, was dumped via text, became a missing person, and received a handful of speculations, including bipolarity, an allergy to gluten, severe panic disorder, and ADHD. With the inconsistent ideas conjured up about me and my spells, the doctors might as well have thrown darts at a smorgasbord of a half-million diagnoses for my disorder or disease.

Maybe there is nothing wrong with me, and I just have out-of-body experiences. So what? Who needs labels anyway? So what if I've failed? I guess it isn't in God's plan. I've heard God doesn't like psychics, so that could be why.

Is Max still mad? Did he really move out, or is he bluffing? With my bags packed and pills in tow, I'm ready to go back to Dallas, defeated.

Pecos, Texas

9:43 a.m.

Orlando James, 32

You're fucking stupid, Orlando. How could you have run out of gas on your way home? You shoulda stopped for gas when you saw that one stupid station right when your light came on. You know there's only a single gas station for every one hundred miles or so out here. You shoulda known better, Orlando. You should open a huge gas station out here! You'll look into this project when you get home. There's nothing to make you feel more powerless and stupid than running out of gas in the middle of nowhere, with few drivers even passing by. You're lucky it's not hot out, probably only eighty. You hear someone coming, maybe. It is! You try and wave them down. They don't stop, the wretched cunts! You flip them off. Assholes in their stupid-ass minivan. You need to let them know how you feel about them.

"Fuck you. You're such a bunch of losers with your sticker stick family on your window! I hope you get into a car accident and die! And your daughter's ugly!" Yes, you feel better. Hopefully, they heard you. Maybe you should stick your thumb out like they did in the seventies.

You're getting hungry, and the water left in your liter is dwindling. You keep walking, hoping for service to come through on your Android so you can figure out your next move. You hear someone coming. Stick your thumb out like they did in the seventies! Here comes someone!

Poppy

"Hey, where you going?" I ask, rolling down my window. I am in the euphoria stage of another attack, though mild. I still think it would be a good idea to give this guy a ride. The euphoria is quick, though, and now I can't just drive off and leave this bloke out here. Plus he's kinda cute. The tedious roads give me a craving for adventure, or at least someone to talk to. Similarly attractive and gritty, he wears a white T-shirt, jeans, boots, and a baby beard. I glance at his near-empty water jug, deciding he can't be harmful, because the temperature is warming and no civilization can be found. Therefore, it wouldn't make sense for him to be interested in wasting his energy—or electrolytes—by raping or murdering me.

"Um, hey. Tucson. You? Well, really just a gas station, but I can't get service on my fucking phone, because we're literally in the middle of nowhere. You got service on your phone?"

"Actually, I got mad at my ex and threw it out the window…I dunno, a couple hundred miles back."

"Ha! Well, we make one hell of a duo out here, huh? I don't have gas; you don't have a phone." He leans in, giving me his full attention, obviously grateful I stopped, but doesn't thank me. I'm not sure whether manners are a thing in hitchhiker culture.

Luckily, I don't have an appointment to go to, just back home, out on that open road.

"You ran out of gas? Aren't you going the wrong way?"

"Well, technically yes, but I think I passed a station about four miles back, was gonna hit that up since I dunno how many miles to the next one." He lights a cigarette he has hidden behind his ear.

"Oh, well, maybe I can give you a quick ride…"

"What you doing out here, girl? I like that shirt, by the way," the weirdo tells me. It's a good thing he's cute, because if you're not cute, you need to be smart and/or nice, and he's probably neither.

"Poppy."

"Poppy, hi. I'm Orlando. Nice to meet you." He extends his hand through the passenger window. His fingernails are dirty. We chat about the weather and how the "no gas station" policy for sixty miles is a real drag. He tells me he's going to open a gas station out here. He leans in my car, getting more comfortable with my car as a prop to hold him up. Soon he might just fold himself through the window. He talks a lot, and rapidly, so much so I can barely understand what he says for a couple of words. He's telling me his ideas about a gas station and how it's going to be the most amazing one in the world, with restroom attendants who clean the toilet when you leave and before you get there and wait for you to finish washing your hands so they can hand you a napkin and a mint. Maybe even a shot of tequila, then mouthwash to hide any evidence. He's even using his hands to paint a better mental picture in my mind. I gotta love people with a passion for talking.

"I was visiting my, how should I say, baby mama." This is disappointing, but I don't want to mess with someone with seventeen years of baggage ahead of him. He goes on to talk shit about his baby mama but swoons and lights up over his son.

He looks inside and judges the empty water bottles and hunter-green Starbucks sticks that I use as toothpicks. He has long eyelashes and dark eyes, so he must be laced with

Italian, Middle Eastern, or Latin blood. It's refreshing to have a semienlightening conversation with a male, and since he needs a ride, I'm basically stuck with him, like a stray dog that won't stop following you once you pet it, trying to go home with you. He could be mad; only time will tell. Anyone who talks that quickly and isn't on meth has a ticker in his head; think Kanye.

"Okay, well, I gotta get going. Good luck!" I say, rolling up my window, exhausted by his verbal explosion. This way he knows I'm serious about leaving. Plus he has a kid and is *clearly* irresponsible. No, thanks.

Chapter 13

O Part Deux

"Wait!" he yells. I release the window.

"Yes?"

"I need gas. Would you mind giving me a ride? Please? I'm desperate here. I've been trying, and there was this minivan cunt family with one of those God-awful stick-family stickers. They didn't stop. You're the second car to come by in fifteen minutes, so I would—"

"Put your hands on your head and turn around."

He complies and looks confused.

"Empty your pockets," I order. I'm not about to get mugged or killed by some cute hitchhiker. Is he really cute, though, or am I blinded by boredom? He does talk too much though; it'd probably drive me crazy. Imagine what your fights would look like! He rolls his eyes and pulls his pockets out of his faded jeans, revealing only white cotton.

"There, you happy?"

"Lift up your shirt."

"Are you fuck—"

"You want a ride or not?"

"Your sanity, huh?" he asks, trying to decide whether I'm serious.

"Those who have nothing to hide, hide nothing!" I say, repeating Dr. Phil. He has a chiseled stomach for a pool-service equipment owner and operator and a future gas station empire CEO.

"Anything else?"

"Nah, get in."

"Thanks!" He opens the passenger door and throws out his hand. Now that we're side by side, he smells like dirty tobacco and dust. I get back on the road, heading eastbound on I-20.

"Where you goin' anyway? Need a fix?" he asks.

"A fix of what?"

"Heroin. You looking for the Farm?"

"No! Wait, what farm? I'm confused."

"They call it Contin Farm. Some sort of secret society where heroin addicts hang out and get high all day. Get it? Contin like Oxy—"

"Yeah, I get it. So it's a trap house?"

"Yeah, sort of, except they don't use cash. Everything revolves around drugs. They use heroin, like, in lieu of cash. I think they work with the Mexican drug cartels somehow." I almost slam on my brakes in shock, remembering those people and E & J's who mentioned this and I thought they were crazy.

"Oh my God, I heard people talking about that! Where is it? Do you know how to get there from here?"

"Yeah, of course. Made this drive a few times."

"Oh, so you're an addict? Great."

"Fuck no. Can't stand the shit. Or junkies really. I just come this way from Midland, and I see them all strung out on the side of the highway sometimes. I guess they go for highway strolls or something. Maybe looking for money. Or men. Truckers. Yeah, I bet they fuck a ton of truckers through here."

"Can we go?"

"Why? Didn't you say you didn't do heroin?"

"No, I don't, but I have a background in, shall we say, addiction."

"Oh yeah? Like what? They say everyone there started with OxyContin or Percocet or some other pain med they got from an injury. Now they're all full-fledged junkies, working and getting paid in dope."

I tell Orlando about my alcohol and Xanax history, how I got sober, and what I do to maintain sobriety.

"It's a baffling thing, addiction. The only disease those affected don't actually believe they have."

"I know. Trust me, I get it," he says, pulling out a cigarette.

"Um, excuse me," I say, rolling down his window.

"Oh, mind if I smoke?" he asks with a wink.

"Whatever. Just keep that shit outside the whole time. Like I want your arm to be so far out the window…who even smokes anymore anyway?"

"Um, me."

"You get what, by the way?"

"Come again?"

"You said a second ago you get it. Are you in recovery or anything?"

"Nope!" He tells me about his deceased twin brother, who choked on his own vomit after a night of binge drinking. He says his brother knew he was an alcoholic but said the steps didn't work.

"Oh my God. I'm so sorry. That's awful."

"It's all right. He's in a better place now, I suppose. Finally drank himself to death."

"Geez. When did that happen?"

"About a year ago. I mean, it was *his* fucking choice, you know? I mean, what did he *think* would happen if he drank twelve shots? We tried to get him help for years. He got sent away and shit, dozens of times."

"I know it's rough. Addiction is rough. It's like, well, you will *never* find anyone diagnosed with colon cancer leaving a doctor's office denying they have cancer, even if they have all of the symptoms and positive test results. They don't think they get a pass because they're too young, pretty, old, smart, rich, or dumb to have cancer and therefore don't need to follow a chemo regimen because it's inconvenient. They listen to their doctor's orders because they know cancer doesn't go away on its own and to be free of an ailment, it takes some effort and acceptance."

"Yep!" he says, exhaling white fog. "Never thought of it like that. Shit, take this next exit. I'll go with you, but I don't wanna stay for too long."

"Okay, great."

He flicks his cigarette out the window.

"That's littering," I remind him. He rolls his eyes, and I take the exit he says to, curious to learn how a tiny world operates solely off heroin, if it is, in fact, true.

We pass an uneventful Motel 6 and vacant restaurants serving fried chicken and an adobe church built before the Mexican Revolutionary War. Cactuses are widely dispersed, and the silence is alarming.

"Take a right at the light."

We pass a green rectangle sign that pops in contrast to all the brown and yellow:

Van Horn

Population: 2,362

To live in a city with fewer than three thousand people requires a genuine love for simplicity and silence, a place that seems counterintuitive to a heroin-bartering ranch.

"VAAAAAAANNNNNN Horn!" says Orlando in a pitiful southern accent, cupping his mouth as he leans against the car door.

"I don't get it."

"Get what, shuga?" He looks around, amused.

"How people can live in a town this small. What do they do all day? It's fascinating.

"What is?"

"People's perception of excitement."

"Well, lessseee. You got your ranchers, farmers maybe, or is it too dry? You got to have someone to work at that café over yonder and the hotel and…shit, I dunno."

"I'd go crazy."

Chapter 14

The Arrival

A middle-aged woman with frizzy blond hair wearing a fanny pack with wrinkled, thin legs in frayed denim shorts three sizes too big looks at us and walks in our direction. She furrows her brow and pouts her lips in curiosity.

"She looks real nice," says Orlando.

"And hungry. Where do you get food around here? That one single street with the cheap hotels?"

"Follow this road. See that house up there? I think that's it." He points to what was once a nice Victorian family home and is now in forlorn ruins. A couple of shingles are missing off the roof, a window shutter is gone, and the paint is peeling. The opposite of what you'd imagine a billionaire heiress to have, if it is, in fact, true. By the looks of it, I'm sure it's a straight-up trap house. Orlando has to be confused. A beautiful Latina appears from the back, riding a bike and wearing headphones, so she doesn't hear us right away since her back is to us. I creep up the hill anxiously.

"Damn, she's an addict? She's gorgeous," says Orlando. There are two guys around my age who appear to be lying on the ground on the opposite side of the multiacreage property, soaking in the sun, making snow angels as a young woman is smoking and watching them. She has some sort of leg injury. She laughs at them and sees us. The Latina on the bike finally notices us and pedals off like a frightened deer, her supersize breasts leading the way, almost pulling her down.

"Here, park over there. I think that's, like, the owner," Orlando says, beginning to panic. "Dammit, why are we here?" He rubs his eyes.

"Because you ran out of gas," I remind him, "and I didn't."

"Look, they see us. They're probably getting their AKs."

Empty Twinkie wrappers, soda bottles, boxes of foil, lighter, spoons, syringes, packs of cigarettes, and tiny orange lids litter the ground.

"Guess they don't believe in trash cans here, either," I say.

"Yeah, by the looks, it definitely doesn't look like they believe in much."

I park my car, and the two men, the girl, the Latina, and now a black man start walking toward my car, about a thousand feet away.

"Should we get out or…"

"I mean, we're here now, yeah? This was your idea, so let's check it out," says Orlando, opening the car door.

We start walking toward them, eyeing the mountains in the distance.

The Latina, still on the bike, uses caution when riding to avoid running over a desert bush or glass bottle.

"How far away are we from Marfa?" I ask to ease the tension.

"Probably an hour or so. Please God, don't tell me you're going there next."

"Well, I'd like to check it out,"

"Okay, then, on our way there, the moment I get service, I'm jumping out of your car."

Orlando waves to the Latina.

"Hi, can we help you?" I notice the shiny .44 Mag in her white wicker basket, next to a pink bell.

Chapter 15

Ocielle

Ocielle Rodriguez, 25

You don't know why this couple is here, but it's probably for that shit Carlos brings that junkies hear about, that makes these white people cum. Shirley is out today. She's your dominant personality. She's a middle-aged woman from East Texas who's always saying inappropriate and vulgar things. She has a twang to her voice. Nowhere in America do you see willing and capable white and black men and women bowing down and working for a Latina, except here. This is Contin Farm. These are your bitches, and now it looks like you just got two more. You wonder what their trade is. Are they cooks, cleaners? Can they give massages or clean the pool? You wonder if the guy is a plumber. You need someone who's good at plumbing to live here. These other people suck at it. How hard could it be? These are better than Facebook "friends" that everyone has. These are *your* homies. They worship you; they love you. All you have to do is give them heroin when they do their work. No need for cash. Junkies only get and keep cash for ten seconds anyway, until it slides out of their dirty hands and into the dirtier hand of a dealer. You simply cut out the middleman.

You have the power, Shirley. You make the lists; you make the rules; you do it all. Really, *you're* an entrepreneur, and you did it without your daddy's help. A businesswoman is still a businesswoman, even if it's an "illegal American" business. Americans do illegal shit all the time; it's just easier (and cheaper) to catch a drug dealer than an identity thief, a tax evader, or a bribing attorney. But all the friends and parties you never got to have (or attend) because your father was the highest-ranking drug aficionado of the nineties, and because kidnapping was almost a certainty, you do every day now! Your peers you *were* so envious of have dead-end jobs they hate but work their asses off to keep and babies to pay for. If they could see you now. No more of the hidden kingpin spawn, hiding in the shadows, going to weekly funerals with a black veil always covering your face. Your dad can't hold you back anymore.

It would make him nervous if he knew how many friends you have! He would be convinced they wanted to kill you or rob you, but they don't…you don't think. You suddenly feel very apprehensive about the couple and their motives. You crouch low. Sadie, the five-year-old, has come out.

You stick your thumb in your mouth for comfort. You want your mommy. They're coming closer…quick, run! You run to the porch. You need Agnes, your doll. You run upstairs to get her. She's sitting on your bed, waiting for you. Now you should ride your bike. You can put Agnes in the basket! You feel better now that Agnes is with you. Maybe these strangers will be nice to you and want to be your friend. You pedal around for a few minutes in a circle, reciting the ABCs and singing "The Itsy-Bitsy Spider."

Yesenia, the thirty-four-year-old attorney, joins in. Pharmaceutical companies and doctors set the ball rolling for most of your friends and roommates, not the cartels, and certainly not you. You've always been surrounded by drugs and people doing them since you can remember. Your funniest memory is when you were six or seven and couldn't find your huge teddy bear, Sammy, so you could go to sleep. You found it under one of your dad's "friends," who fell asleep on it with a needle in his arm. You remember him because he had blue lips. You yanked Sammy from under the blue man, and he didn't flinch. You washed off his drool and went soundly to sleep.

You glance down at your three-carat sapphire ring your dad gave you for graduation and your pointy red nails. You need to send someone to get you more of that Chanel hand cream your mom has used for decades and swears by.

Yes. I bet they're just customers. The gringo man is tall, pretty handsome in a plain white T-shirt and jeans. La gringa is wearing denim shorts and a green T-shirt with something on it. You wonder if they're fucking or if they're brother and sister. She is pretty; he is pretty. They must be baby addicts. Fresh meat. New to the game.

Chapter 16

Prince

Prince White, 42

You're too old for this shit, Prince. You should be with your family, but instead you've
fallen for the devil's advertisement and are wasting your days away with these junkie
kids going nowhere, not even giving themselves the opportunity to try. But you, you had
a great job, a beautiful wife, and (previously) healthy children. More than what most
could ask for. You want to shout to the couple to get back in their car and go home to
their families before it's too late. When you get to Contin Farm, there's only one place
to go from here: a nice, shiny hole. But that's all heroin is, anyway: a bottomless pit you
can't get out of until you quit or die. Did you forget to turn your bedroom light off? You
used the stove last night. Dammit, you need to go check. This bitch is about to burn to
the ground because of you! You go back in before your anxiety takes the wheel.

You have things to do, but here you go again with your rituals you started as a kid, and
you still haven't seen a doctor. During your teenage years, you avoided going to the zoo,
being around babies (especially animals) out of fear you were going to randomly snap
and choke them and kill them or bash their skulls in with a hammer. You asked your
mom if she could hide all of the tools in your house. A couple years ago, you slept in
handcuffs attached to your bed frame out of fear you were going to jump out of the
window and commit suicide. Your wife started to become distant, tired of your rituals,
making you late to things like church, work, and meeting with friends and family.

You even got let go from your last job as a textile worker because you had to constantly
go back to your house and check that the coffeepot was off, that there were no traces of
food particles in the sink, and when you left, you had to lead with your left foot of each
step *always*, and if you messed up, you did it again, and you could only drive in a certain
spot in every center lane. Your wife didn't understand why you couldn't relax. If you
told her you were afraid you were going to kill her and Johnny in the middle of the
night, she would simply reply, "No, you're not," and go about her day. Didn't she know

you were a potential murderer? When you got injured on the job and were given a prescription of Percocet, your anxiety and OCD went away. All emotion went away, and you couldn't stay away from the luxury and benefit of not having crippling anxiety and rituals and compulsions. You were your old self again, better than you could remember. Lately, they haven't been doing their job, which is concerning you.

You check the lights in the house, count your steps, and wonder what injury brought those kids here, or who. Lord Jesus, please curse the doctors who are getting these kids started down the wrong path because they don't know better.

Truth is, not all addicts have the pleasure of dying from an overdose like your son, Johnny. Johnny boy. God, you miss him. He was a smart kid, a good leader, made the honor roll throughout high school, loved sports. He really loved it all, and everyone loved him. Got into the University of Texas and was planning on going last fall. Since the overdose, he doesn't know where or who he is, and that's your fault. No, actually, you didn't formulate those circumstances; that was God. It's God's fault your boy is a vegetable because he took too strong a dose and couldn't get oxygen to his brain, but it didn't kill him.

Don't you blame God, Prince! Even if you don't understand why you used to get up and go to church every Sunday and show up for him, but when you need him, he's MIA. You know God is the alpha and the omega and can heal the blind to see, but why can't he fix you?

There must be a reason, and the reason is this: if you really had a problem, your Lord would save you, and since he hasn't—all is well. You just couldn't handle the grief of your boy, turning your compulsions into overdrive. You suddenly couldn't get out of bed until you counted all of the ceiling tiles. When you ate breakfast, your cereal bag or box could never touch the bowl, or you had to throw it away. The milk had to face a certain way in the fridge, and so on. All day long.

Grief—that makes you feel more powerless than a mosquito on an ice cap. He was saved from death, and grateful you are, but he will never be the same. You're not sure you made the right decision to keep him alive; that's always something you debate over in your mind. The doctors say his brain will never recuperate from seconds of oxygen loss when he overdosed. The same doctors who probably wrote him his prescription for opiates from a football injury who said they'd help him deal with his back pain. Then y'all began sharing pills, and things got sticky. You believe he can come back one day, since the doctors were wrong once and they can be wrong again.

No, don't blame your using or John's on doctors, Prince. You got yourself into this mess; now here you are. Livin' for free with a crazy Mexican girl who fucks a cartel boy—and gives away heroin for the return of our "friendship," in a mansion that looks like Section 8 housing on the outside and the Taj Ma-fucking-hal on the inside. You've heard her father is some bigwig motherfucker in the cartel, yet your girl Ocielle would rather be out in the middle of a West Texas desert and take care of us junkies. Bless that Ocielle, but how can someone be so naïve?

Chapter 17

Welcome to Contin Farm

Contin Farm, Van Horn, Texas

10:54 a.m.

"Oh, hi, I'm Poppy, and this is Orlando." Orlando waves.

"Okay, hi, I'm Ocielle. How can I help you?" she asks again and adjusts her black crop top over her enlarged breasts, which match her enhanced butt. I'm unsure of what to say when, gratefully, her phone starts to ring before I can respond.

"Excuse me," says Ocielle, grabbing her phone from her basket. "Bueno? Hola bebé. ¿Lo tienes? ¿Estás bien? Perfecto. Tengo algunos nuevos clientes aquí…creo. No sé lo que quieren, no. ¿Quizás medio kilo? Eso debería durar un tiempo, apuesto. Sí, sí, puedes ponerlo en cualquier lugar. ¿Cuarenta y cinco? Está bien te veo pronto adios."

Likely on the phone with a customer or dealer, she speaks about kilos of something, he will be over in forty five minutes, and he can put it anywhere.

"Sorry. What can I do for you?" she asks.

"Well, we were just passing through and saw this…amazing house! I'm currently building and was looking for some design and architectural ideas," I say. One of the worst lies I've told lately.

"Oh." She sounds surprised. "Well, it needs some work, but you can go look on the inside if you like."

"Okay, thank you so much!" I say, shooting a sinister grin at Orlando. Ocielle pedals off, and I'm amazed how easy that was. She yells "PRINCE!" while riding back to the house. We inadvertently follow her trail when an older, sharply dressed black man comes out of the unfenced backyard.

"Hi!" I say.

"Well, hello. How…might…we…be able…to assist…you today?" he asks, super high and barely able to keep his eyes open. He also has a fanny pack on that doesn't match with his Brooks Brothers style.

"Um, well, we're just here to—"

"See the circus," interrupts Orlando.

"I beg…your…pardon?"

"He's lying. We were just passing through and saw this old house sitting all alone."

"We're looking for architecture ideas," says Orlando.

It is hard to think of something to say when you're intentionally trespassing on someone's property and have no reason for visiting. Prince's mood shifts from helpful to suspicious.

"Let's…not…dick…around, you…two. Do…you…need…to get high?" He almost trips on his freshly polished leather loafers.

"No," we say simultaneously, looking at each other.

"We really don't," I add. He tells us his name's Prince and he's from Knoxville. I get out a Valium from my bag to, hopefully, prevent an attack. I feel the sudden rush of anxiety, spurred by Prince, how high he is, and his pristine outfit, and also the fact I'm on the property of a stranger who has a gun in her basket and huge fake body parts.

"Would you like…a…tour?" We nod.

"Thank you, that would be great," I say and follow Prince's turtle pace to the house. "You live here, I assume?" I ask.

"Yep! Rent-free. Well, not a hundred percent free, but you know what I'm sayin'."

"Yeah. How long have you been here?" Orlando asks.

"Um, what month are we in?"

"May."

"And it's 2015, so I've been here about…maybe a little over a year, I suppose."

One of the window shutters is destined to drop at any moment, the upper right window had a run-in with a bowling ball, and the shingles are faded and thinning. You could easily find a house similar to it listed online as a "rural renovator's dream."

"So this is Contin Farm," says Prince, gripping the digital door handle, "where…about…let's see…Kurt, Marilyn, Jimi, me, Ocielle, Amy, Janis…seven people live." He counts on his fingers.

"Cotton Farm?" I ask.

"No child, Con*tin* Farm, and…I think 'farm' should be spelled…like…p-h-pharmacy. Get it?" Prince says with a laugh.

"Yeah, Poppy, like OxyContin," says Orlando.

"There you go. Just like OxyContin. Y'know…he's…a pretty…smart…young man. You did good, young lady," he says, smiling and looking at me. "The devil's…drug. Welcome…to the Farm, y'all."

Our jaws drop when we see the guts of Contin Farm.

Chapter 18

Carlos

Carlos Saucedo "Burro Grande" Mendoza, 25

You're excited to see OC. You haven't seen her in a while; you think it's because some people have left the house her dad gave her or she's cutting the doses back, like you asked her, so the boss doesn't get suspicious. Hopefully she's in a Shirley or Yesenia mood. It's strange when she talks to you in a baby voice and needs her stuffed doll when you have sex.

Luckily, the boss hasn't found you in the supply freezer after hours. You want to someday make a real career, but the Mexican government leaves you powerless with no choice but to sell narcotics. You are in love with OC, but if her father knew you were sleeping with her, he would cut your head off and hang it on his wall, and every night before he went to the sleep, he would get to see the last look of pain, fear, and blood in your eyes before he cut off your head with his execution chainsaw.

You have to live this life, to sell heroin and kill anyone who tries to take your customers. When you were a kid, you wanted to be a police officer. Now you're on the opposite side of the tracks. The side you never thought you would be on until you met some people who offered a way out of poverty to you and your family. No more sleeping in cars, selling fruit, riding bicycles, no electricity. Your parents have a house on the coast and live nice. That makes you happy.

It's funny to you how Americans get upset talking about "terrorists" and how they shoot people in the nightclubs and everyone is so shocked. In Mexico that happens all the time; it's just a normal day to you and your friends and narcos. The "radicals" of ISIS are choir bitch boys compared to what goes on in Juarez and Sinaloa.

You cross paths with other cartels and you die, or your family members die if they don't find you. You're putting your life on the line to see her, because sooner or later the boss man is going to wonder where the kilo is and will kill all the donkeys, including you, the *burro grande, si él no puede encontrar.*

It's hard for you to visit Ocielle; it's because you just *sexo* and leave. You want her to come back to Juarez, back to her family, her mom, *tías, tíos, primos, sobrinos, nietos,* amigos, and everyone. You can all be a family. You think she learned from her American nanny it's okay to leave your family behind, but in Mexico that is not okay. She is probably messed up in the head she gets from her mom. She dated a white man; Dad disapproved. You hear he is missing, but you and Ocielle know what happened to him.

The baggies under your foot and in your layers of socks are making you hot, and you regret the decision not to rope it to your testicles. You pull into OC's driveway and see a car there you haven't seen. You get worried and speed faster down the long dirt driveway.

Chapter 19

Guts

The foyer is massive, with marble walls and tile, and is shockingly bright. A massive crystal chandelier hangs from the ceiling, glistening in the sun from a broken window. Framed prints and original artworks decorate the walls, including a Jackson Pollock painting.

"Wow, this is nice," I say.

"Here's the living area," says Prince. On the gold coffee table are two syringes, some foil, and a spoon, next to a pipe. "Please excuse our mess. I guess some people don't know how to clean up after themselves."

"This is gorgeous," I say, ignoring Prince and eyeing the details from the layered crown molding to the huge flat screen that comes down from upstairs. A pair of Louboutin heels lies on the Persian rug. Surround sound throughout the house is currently playing classical music. I feel the Valium kicking in, and I'm thrilled as a sensory overload is happening; my spells love this kind of stuff. The kitchen smells like a mixture of fresh tortillas and coffee.

"So she or someone doesn't believe in the upkeep of the outside, just the inside?" I ask, confused, remembering the broken windows along with the falling shutters and torn roof to match the hanging gutter pipes.

"I guess…yeah…you know. This way…the house blends in…around here. We do some private stuff around here, and you don't want strangers like you always coming by to admire the place, so Ocielle needs to fool…any…outsiders…you know, for our protection."

Orlando rolls his eyes.

Family photos in thick gilded frames are all over the house. In the kitchen there's a photo of Ocielle sexually holding a leash to a tiger, wearing a minidress with a gun buckled into her stiletto. An espresso machine, marble countertops, a bowl of fruit, and shiny stainless steel appliances complement one another. I head back to the foyer.

"So where does she work?" I ask Prince, knowing the answer, but it sounds good to ask. He's telling Orlando the features of the kitchen.

"Oh, child. You don't know?" Prince lowers his voice to a whisper and walks toward me to whisper in my ear.

"Her dad is one…of…the founders…of the…largest…and most violent…drug cartels in Mexico. She doesn't need to work a day in her life. She's a billionaire…drug giver-slash-dealer…heiress." Orlando's gaze is fixed on the elaborate marble ceiling tiles that spell out "Rodriguez" in gold.

"Oh really?" I ask. Prince leads us down a hall going who knows where, and I hear what sounds like someone wringing a mop and plopping it down on the floor. The door is shut, and on the outside it reads "Caution. Tiger on Premises." I cover my mouth and look at Orlando.

"Holy shit, there's not really a tiger in there," I ask, looking at Prince.

"Oh, yes, ma'am, Missy girl. She's Ocielle's pet. I think Kurt has the duty of cleaning her room today. Sounds like he's mopping in there now."

"That's messed up. Tigers aren't pets!" I whisper aggressively.

"No, they're definitely not, but having a tiger…to them…represents a level of superiority."

"Such bullshit," says Orlando.

"So her dad bought her this house?" I ask as we walk farther down the hallway to the swimming area.

"Yeah. I heard they cut ties when she started dating a white guy, and he told her she could have the house but get out. Spent close to a million on it, I wanna say."

"Damn. Just so she can get high and not worry about life?"

Prince stops walking to tell us (slowly) how the system of the house works and that

Ocielle herself doesn't use heroin, since she has to "take care of it, when really she just needs to take care of us dope fiends. We're really pretty simple, now that I think about it. We just need one thing, and one thing only, and we good," Prince says, patting his fanny pack.

"She doesn't do shit though. We the ones who run the household," he says. She gets her supply from a Mexican cartel guy called Carlos, who's associated with her father's cartel. It is the wildest business partnership in existence, centering on the one thing that's the center of their universe.

Simultaneously, Janis, Prince, Kurt, Jimi, Amy, and Marilyn are her employees *and* her "friends." Ocielle sometimes cooks for them, Prince tells us. She thrives on their approval, their admiration, their glorification, and the Chanel deliveries they are responsible for if they want dope. She is the ultimate codependent and loves it.

To get the dope their bodies need to avoid withdrawal, they are required to perform duties not limited to cleaning the house and polishing the silver, running out to get her dry cleaning, taking care of Missy, getting Ocielle's favorite snacks, making her appointments, paying her bills, stealing or selling heroin to get extra cash, and picking up shipments from the post office, which more often than not contain clothing she ordered online. Heroin shipments are delivered to the house via Carlos or hauled in on a semidisguised truck with a chain toy store logo from across the border. The amounts of heroin the tenants receive depend on the chores they do.

"And she pays y'all?" asks Orlando.

"Hell…yeah. In…dope, my brother," says Prince. He knocks on a closed door and puts his ear to it. When I glance up at the ornate crown molding throughout, I notice two surveillance cameras pointed toward the room entrance. On the wall outside of her bedroom hang Polaroids of twenty or so people I assume are her wide circle of friends. Some are old, some teenagers, all races, sizes, and creeds. Some look blissfully happy while others look as if they are struggling.

"She's not here. She won't care, I bet. After all, I cleaned it for her this mornin'!" Prince opens the door to reveal a room I would assume belonged to Gianni Versace.

"Ho…ly…shit," whispers Orlando.

"Amazing, right? Lucky…little bitch, I tell ya," Prince mumbles, looking around slowly.

The walls are beautifully painted with biblical scenes, a life-size angel playing a violin and looking at baby Jesus while other angelic humans gather around under a perfectly blue sky with vast pear trees spreading onto the ceiling. The classical music playing certainly makes it seem like heaven, except with heroin addicts. Her silk king-size bedspread is gold with mink pillows, and an ornately carved, at least four-foot-high headboard matches the china cabinet across the room.

The bathroom is just as extravagant, including a Jacuzzi and a shower meant for five, with a walk-in closet big enough to live in comfortably.

"Prince!" we hear someone call from downstairs.

"Shit, that's her, I bet. Better get a move on. Yes?" he calls back.

"Out of my room, please," she yells from downstairs. "You know I only like you in there if y'all are cleaning. Are you cleaning?"

"Um, no, I is just showing our guests—"

"Then get the fuck out!"

"Should we leave?" I ask Prince, almost frightened of what she is capable of.

"Nah, she's fine. Lemme show you the pool." He leads us into another room, though this one is a room with a pool and thick marble columns.

"No shit," mutters Orlando, putting his phone away as he tries to get service in every room.

"Yeah, sometimes she'll let us swim, but she usually reserves it for her suitors, and Marilyn."

Prince says Marilyn is Ocielle's best (living) girlfriend she likes the most, so they stick together like glue. Prince takes us to a theater room with massage chairs that seat ten.

Back downstairs in the kitchen, a blond female is hovering over the kitchen table, which seats twenty. Her hair hangs over her face, and she doesn't seem to notice or care that Prince, Orlando, and I are here.

Prince gets an apple from the fruit spread. The doorbell rings. Orlando seems concerned about the blonde, who hasn't moved. Upstairs we hear Ocielle yell, "Got it!"

Chapter 20

Le Tigre and the Fornication

Missy

Mmm, fresh meat. Maybe. Are they for you? Usually one of the keepers gives you your raw meat in a bowl, not still walking around and talking! Oh well, you can take them down if they *are*, in fact, your dinner. Women humans are fattier, so you'll eat the girl first, have her man human as a snack later. You lick your lips and climb up your man-made tree. You scared them away, Missy! Your dinner just left. You're sure they'll come back. Everyone loves to look at you and see what you're doing, like, hey, I'm just over here napping, not that exciting, leave me alone. Your tail itches, so you climb down from your fake tree and scratch it. Yes. That's better. Damn tail. You're kind of tired. Yes, it's nap time for you. You get a drink of water from your pool for kids / water bowl and lie down, stretching out your limbs.

That always feels nice.

No visitors, please.

You yawn big. Your face is dirty; you lick your paw and wipe it.

Close your eyes. You dream of chasing antelopes. Powerless, silly, timid creatures who try and outrun the king of kings. They put up a good fight though, and kitty, aren't they juicy.

Poppy

Ocielle's perfume arrives before she does. "Excuse me," she says to Prince, Orlando, and me, walking through our tour of her four-thousand-square-foot house. She opens the front door wearing a red bustier top, leather leggings, and suede platforms. Her hair had been washed and curled, her face made up as if she were going to prom.

"Hi, babe!" she says to a sweating Hispanic man in his midthirties wearing a beige T-shirt with white splatters of paint, ripped blue jeans, and work boots. He can't be taller than five feet six, and his mustache gives him the appearance of a working-class man, not a drug mule.

"Wow, look at you!" he says, hugging her. He whispers something in her ear. Ocielle grabs him by the hand and escorts him upstairs. He acknowledges us on his way with a smile and wave and practically skips up the stairs, gently rattling the massive crystal chandelier in the foyer.

"That's Carlos," whispers Prince. A door slams; we can hear them laughing.

"The dealer?" I mouth to Prince.

"Yeah. He usually comes by once a month or so with dope. They have conjugal visitations, and then he heads back to Mexico. I think."

"So she doesn't pay him though, right? I mean, he could easily have half a mil worth of dope in that bag he's got," whispers Orlando.

"Define 'pay.' Like cash?" asks Prince.

"Yes."

"Then no, no cash."

To low-bottom heroin addicts, cash is useless in every other aspect of survival except to buy heroin. They spend an average of $67,000 annually on their habits—give or take, of course—so it behooves them to do chores and run errands for Ocielle (and even receive the occasional verbal lashing from her tyrant tongue), but it beats the hell out of prostituting, stealing from loved ones, living under a bridge or in a shelter, sitting in the pen, or trafficking narcotics wrapped in a condom and then swallowed.

"How was the drive?" Ocielle asks, locking the door.

"Not too bad. Took the express lane, so they rarely check me. You look beautiful, mami," Carlos says, grabbing her waist and kissing her hard.

"Thank you. You don't look bad yourself. How much did you bring me?"

"A key," he says, taking off his shoes, referring to the $75,000 market price for an amount of heroin a little larger than a brick.

Ocielle smiles, not elated but satisfied. Carlos pulls out about ten plastic sandwich baggies from underneath his foot, looking like condoms filled with sand. With every bag he removes from various hidden parts of his body, Ocielle's smile gets wider and wider, as if she's on a game show, winning more and more money.

"Yes, papi!" she squeals. They are in the library of the house, surrounded by built-in bookcases filled with an assortment of books on topics from Mexico to fashion to wars to Socrates. She spins around a bookcase, revealing a safe, and starts typing in a code. She puts the baggies inside, slams the safe shut, checks to make sure it's locked (twice), and spins the bookcase around again. Carlos waits comfortably on the leather fainting couch with his arm behind his head.

"How's Daddy?" she asks.

"Take your top off, and I'll tell you." She obeys and walks over to him, revealing her flesh-covered cantaloupes, perky and vibing like his pants, and starts to play with her cantaloupes.

"He's good. Took out a couple Coronados last week, so we were celebrating."

"How?"

"Um," he says, distracted, "someone got word they were at this club, so we went over there and…took them out."

"Oh shit. Those poor Coronados."

"Yep. Your dad, me, and Delfino got the chainsaw and…removed their heads."

"Oh my God, gross!"

"Yes, it was not pretty. But you don't try and take a route from N3. I mean, come one. Everyone knows that, O. Besides, without taking out the turf dwellers, you wouldn't have all this." He looks around the library with high ceilings, a minibar, and velvet wallpaper. "Make me a drink, yeah?" he says.

"Ay-ay-ay, what you want?"

"Got any Clase?" Carlos is referring to a $1,700 bottle of tequila, Clase Azul Ultra Extra Añejo.

"Let me see. I think so." Her heels clack loudly on the white marble flooring. She pulls out a black ceramic bottle resembling a mix between a skinny flower vase and a school bell at the base. Still topless, Ocielle grabs ice from the minifridge and pours the rich beverage over the ice.

After half an hour of rolling in the hay, a naked Ocielle turns to her naked partner lying next to her, misty and satisfied and sipping his highbrow tequila. "I'm hungry," she says. "Who should make us dinner?"

"I'd go with…whoever is probably the least messed up and the best cook," Carlos says, playing with his thick gold rosary.

"Me," Ocielle says, giggling.

"Why don't you charge them, *mija*? You could make a fortune."

"Are you serious? They don't have anything to their names. They are heroin addicts." Carlos rolls his eyes.

"They help me, really. They clean the house, do the dishes. Like, I haven't cleaned in…a couple years or so. Plus I like to keep my hands clean. I'll be damned if I end up locked up. In and out of prison, no thanks. These are my friends, though. I supply; they clean and run my errands, even sell if I need the extra cash."

"For what? Your dad gives you what? Four thousand a month, right?"

"Yeah, but I need things. Like…a Givenchy bag, Chanel…everything, car maintenance stuff, food. Four thou doesn't always make the cut, so when it doesn't, I sell from your oh-so-generous donations," she says, feeling her tequila shot and rubbing his leg.

"I know you don't get anything delivered here, right?"

"Oh, hell no. You think I'm an idiot? I also send them in town to pick up my purchases from the post office in El Paso once a week. It all works, Carlos. I'm only distributing, not intending to sell. It's different laws. Consider it…charity work," she says.

"*Niña*, get me some of that cash. You know sooner or later Juanito's going to wonder where the money is. Then he'll tell your dad, and it'll all just—"

"Okay, well, you tell him that Ocielle's pussy is better than money. You hungry?" she asks, putting her clothes back on.

"Nah. Got another delivery."

"Where?"

"Sweetwater."

"Damn, that's far."

"Yeah, but I need to make the big monies. I don't make *any* coming here. In fact, I'm losing money," he says, walking over to her. He grabs her ass and kisses the back of her neck. "But it's worth it," he whispers. His mustache tickles her neck, and his hot breath vibrantly smells of aged tequila.

Chapter 21

Marilyn

Marilyn Bateman, 24

You're hope you're not drooling, since these new people are in the room. Whatever, live your life. This is Contin Farm, for God's sake, a heroin commune. Carlos got good smack, and you are allowed to enjoy it. Possess your body. Even though it's fat and disgusting.

Take you over.

You feel the warmth in your fingers and toes, like taking a delicious hot bath from the freezing cold that is life. The warming goes up your legs, now your stomach, breasts, throat, to the top of your head. Here's the exhilaration, like you're about to drop from the world's tallest roller coaster. Your head has fallen forward, and you see your scars on your thighs from cutting as a teenager. You flip your arms over to look at them. From wrist to elbow, there are twenty-seven scars on each arm. You accidentally drool on them, feeling the rush.

You moved into Contin Farm, you'd guess, two years ago now. Time flies when you're high. You needed to get out of Los Angeles, entertaining the sugar daddies for plastic surgery and pills, until you discovered you could entertain the surgeon instead. Go straight to the source for Oxys. Nail him while he's still married; then use the recording from the night you made love for blackmail to get pills. Men can be so stupid.

You learned about Contin Farm via your friend Toby, who is a filmmaker in Marfa. He didn't know you were using when he told you about it, even driving by it to see if it actually existed. You remember that day like it was yesterday. You saw the suited-up black man (Prince), who you thought was a minister. There was an Asian girl here then that was walking with Ocielle in the front, and a redhead and a guy with dreads pedaling in the side yard near the cemetery. It fascinated you, getting a quick glimpse of what it'd be like to have a real family, like they seemed to have at Contin Farm, not a dysfunctional paradise like yours. Your mother, always competing with you, clinging to her youth. An alcoholic, abusive father who's been in and out of prison since you were three, leaving your mom to work around the clock, leaving you and Reagan home alone. One night there was an earthquake, and she wasn't there to protect you and your brother. You sat holding each other, crying, since the already-unstable bunk bed collapsed, and yours landed right on top of your brother's, nearly smushing him to death. You were about seven. Mom was probably working the corner, getting ready to introduce you and your brother to some new bastard that would molest you but that she loved. You told her one day that he played doctor with you and gave you checkups. She didn't think anything of it. You were powerless, afraid to say you didn't like that game, so you complied, thinking it was normal or it was your fault he liked to play that game with you.

Your older brother, Reagan, is a club kid now and an avid costume wearer who lives in Manhattan. He posts pictures of himself kissing men on Facebook yet swears he's straight. He even has a club name of Noodle. Reagan Noodle. He wants everyone to address him as such, while he dresses up in kilts and crop tops with loads of eyeliner and feathered boas, wearing forty women's necklaces, Mardi Gras beads, and a plethora of belts. You're not sure what sort of drugs he's doing, but you think it's either raver drugs or amphetamines. He's nearly forty. He needs to get his life together and stop pretending he's powerless over getting a good-paying job because he "doesn't have the education."

The people on Contin Farm looked normal, not Skid Row-ish. They probably all ate dinner together and sang "Kumbaya." You wanted to feel a part of something, and if something horrible happened, you would have each other there 24-7. You'd never have to be alone again. When you returned to Los Angeles, you announced you were moving to Marfa to get clean and stuffed your clothes in your Prius. It's annoying having to make up stories about your day to your mother, who is usually busier with her own narcissism than her daughter who left one day to "get clean." Not much of a fair statement to call her your mother, because what kind of mother gets her kid a nose job at fourteen? You didn't even have a problem with your nose to begin with, but she did. She said it reminded her of your father's, and it gave her anxiety. She didn't even notice you were doing Oxys. She only noticed if her right breast was bigger than her left or if she really needed calf implants or if she'd get to go out to be seen at 1 Oak or Nobu every weekend with a new guy. Yes, the drug addicts at Contin Farm seemed less dysfunctional than your family, and you wanted to move in as soon as possible.

Chapter 22

Kurt

Kurt Lucciano, 23

You're on your way back to Contin Farm on a Monday afternoon with your boy, Jimi, your best friend on the Farm. You see Carlos's piece of shit 1980-something Camry next to someone's red Mercedes. You roll your eyes. He's going to get killed for doing what he's doing, giving out high-grade tar heroin for pussy. And not just a one-shot-in-the-back-or-head-and-bounce execution. They want their victims to suffer, to be tormented and crucified like Jesus. Please tell me you didn't just compare Carlos to Jesus, Kurt.

You and Jimi have taken Ocielle's M3 BMW to Paso to get it detailed, pick up her clothes she ordered from Chanel at a secret location, sell to some customers, and get her favorite Mexican spring water they don't sell in Van Horn, along with her dry cleaning. It's tricky not to look suspicious in El Paso being two young white guys in an $85,000 car just grabbing some deliveries from a PO box and thirty or so garments from the dry cleaners. You both wear long-sleeve shirts to cover the track marks, so maybe you two aren't dead giveaways as junkies or drug dealers.

You drive slow and cautiously, since you and Jimi just shot up behind some abandoned Pueblo house to make the voyage back to Contin Farm, when Jimi interrupts you.

"Yo, you think if we…actually got busted…Ocielle would come get us…like she says she would?" Jimi asks you. This isn't something you want to think about when you're high. You look at Jimi, who's leaning all the way back in the shiny leather seats, playing with the seat temperature.

"That depends. Maybe. Probably, but…she'd…give…the bail…to Prince or someone who looks…reliable," you say. The dope kicks in, making your eyelids heavier than normal. You go fifty-five and put on the cruise control. "Or she might just be like…'Fuck y'all, white-boy idiots,'" you say.

"Yeah…then…we'd snitch on her and Carlos and be done with that bitch."

You smile at his boldness. "Yeah, until she gets word you did and gets her family cartel members involved. Then that will be the end of us. Well, maybe not you. Think she wants your dick a bit, to be honest," you say, smiling.

"You think? I feel that way about *you* and her," he says, pulling his baseball hat over his eyes.

"We're both pretty good-looking guys, though. I'd say better than average, especially if we got sober and cleaned it all up, you know?"

"Hell yeah. She does like white guys," you say.

"Yeah, so you and her…you could be…her bitch boy, and she'd give you dope, and y'all could live happy ever after out here in…West Texas. You could even, like, teach her to shoot in your neck if you run out of veins, you know," he says, chuckling.

"Yeah, sounds miserable," you add.

You know you need to kick this shit, but you're too much of a pussy to handle withdrawal; plus you haven't had the opportunity to get Suboxone, and treatment's, like, $50,000 and your parents are done with you. Now you're out in some shithole town in Texas doing the same shit *every fucking day* you've done for almost two years now. Wake up, get high, go see what chores need to be done for Queen O, go steal or sell if Her Highness wants some new shoes and blew through her monthly $3,000 allowance already and doesn't have grocery money.

You destroyed your ball-playing scholarship at Duke, so you switched it up geographically and moved to Colorado, where you could snowboard and not worry or obsess about baseball and your career. You kept doing pills when your surgeon prescribed you Percocet after your Tommy John surgery six years ago. You got addicted, and since heroin is easier to find (and cheaper), you switched to that. Four months ago you and your parents looked into rehab for the tenth time. This time it was in Austin, and you were ready.

On the plane you sat next to a guy who told you about Contin Farm. You were feeling worse than terminal with the constant diarrhea, sneezing, runny nose, coughing, shaking, vomiting, and a headache only the devil could give you. Every five minutes you had to get up; luckily, you had an aisle seat. Not wanting to be in pain anymore and have your body secreting liquids from all holes, suddenly you couldn't say no to the idea of an endless, free supply of heroin as long as you did some chores and weren't a scumbag. Unexpectedly, your ambitions to quit and go pro and get your life back on track flew out the six-inch airplane window. You went straight to Van Horn on a Greyhound bus heading to El Paso from the Austin airport.

Why aren't the doctors more to blame? They're the ones who, after you had the Tommy John procedure, put you on all the pain meds in the world and are all, "Good luck with withdrawal and getting into the majors!" Who the hell do they really think needs a sixty-day supply of Percocet? I mean, an athlete with hopes of going pro who had a procedure? Next time, do your fucking research, bro. You got duped.

Chapter 23

Photographs

Prince is strolling around the campus, snapping his fingers and singing or talking to himself. He's wearing a beret and a velvet jacket, exuding style and class. He joins us at the picnic table.

"Whatchall up to over here?" he asks us.

Since Kurt and Jimi are nodding off, Orlando and I respond.

"Oh, nothing. Watching these kids basically die in front of us. Wanna go check out that arcade?" Orlando asks Prince.

"Yeah, sure. You play?"

"I mean...I can. She's got a lot of good ones up there."

"When Carlos leaves. We have to wait."

Prince slides over to the boys, pushing their heads up. Once he pushes up Kurt's forehead with the palm of his hand, he turns around and does the same to Jimi, trying to juggle them to avoid slamming their heads onto the table.

"Hey, fuck off," says Jimi after the third or so push from Prince.

"Yeah, fuck y'all. Got some good shit. Y'all better get it together. You know what happened to my son."

"Your son?" I ask.

"Yeah, long story short, he overdosed but didn't die, but now he's brain dead. A vegetable. Excuse me, y'all," Prince says, opening his fanny pack and getting out a tiny plastic baggie, snorting the white contents.

"Oh my God. I never thought about that," I say. "I mean, I guess it's possible."

"How much longer you think they'll be?" asks Jimi, still with us.

"Who? O and Carlos? He probably gets minimal pussy. I'd say he be good and done by now," says Prince, wiping his nose. "Y'all better make sure you clean up after yourself, now. Don't be leavin' these needles and shit around."

"Well, maybe when we can go inside we can…" says Kurt, with his eyes closed.

"I dunno why y'all do that nasty weird shit anyway. Stick a needle in your arms like you doctors or somethin'."

"Well, I hate to say it, but you're missin' out, bud. Besides, it's either in your arm, up your nose, or in your mouth. Either way, it gets you. Don't matter…the route if it's all going to the same place," says Jimi.

Prince's eyelids start to droop, and he leans back. Orlando throws his arm out for assistance behind him.

"No, Prince, don't ever shoot up. Once you do that, you're chasin'," says Jimi, his head swaying left and right. His voice deepens when he's high.

"Whoa there. Be careful, old man," says Kurt.

"Huh? Oh, did I drift off?"

"Almost."

"I tell ya I didn't sleep none…too…well…last night."

"Or it could be the heroin you just snorted," snips Orlando.

I go inside to grab an apple from the fruit-bowl centerpiece on the island, which Ocielle told me I was welcome to. She is probably wondering how long Orlando and I plan on staying. Since I'd like to arrange an intervention, I have time to fill before my dad and his team can arrive—if he agrees to do it, that is, and if the others don't get suspicious. If I were them, I'd think it quite peculiar a younger woman and a man who weren't users or looking to score would want to spend so much time with those who are.

I need to get more information about the residents and their conditions before I have my dad and his interventionist, Ryan, come out here. Some people are totally fine being addicts—that's the only way of life they claim to identify with, and they don't want to change—and those are the types who die. We cannot help them. There's also the type that's been to several expensive treatment centers, paid for by either their parents or their loved ones. They rack up bills in the $100,000-plus arena just to learn they still aren't ready for sobriety. That type may eventually get (and stay) sober, but the odds are stacked against them.

Then there are the addicts that don't know much about the twelve steps or sobriety but know deep down they need to do *something*. They believe in themselves and know their conditions won't improve once the week is over or spring comes or they get visited by a unicorn who tells them to get help.

However, just because the addict accepts treatment doesn't mean he or she'll stay clean. An overwhelming majority will relapse, and a very low percentage of that majority will stay sober for good and all. These are the ugly facts of addiction.

On my way to the kitchen, I pass by one of the three media rooms, where the door is open and Ocielle is viewing pictures on an old projector. I debate about going in, slightly afraid of catching her off guard and/or pissing her off. The only thing I know about her history is that she's an heiress to one of the most violent drug cartels in Mexico, and potentially with a personality disorder .

"Hey, what are you watching?" I ask nervously, knocking on the door.

"Oh, nothing, just old film reels from my family in Mexico," she says. Her eyes are red as if she's been crying.

"Oh, cool, mind if I watch too?" I ask.

"No, come on in." She's staring at a black-and-white photograph of a girl (I take it to be her) aged around two, wearing a pajama onesie and straddling her shirtless father's legs as she sits on his lap watching television.

"That's my dad and me."

"Cute, what were y'all doing?"

"Umm, probably watching a cartoon. He was a good dad, really. Here, sit down."

Ocielle slaps the leather sofa. Curious to know more about her drug-lord father and mildly afraid of her, I sit quickly.

"Little did I know, the next room and in the closet were bricks of cocaine and marijuana, heroin, all to the ceiling."

In a photo a young woman with dark lips and hair sits in the back seat of an old Chrysler, the window down as she looks curiously out the window. It must have been the early forties.

"Aw, my nana. Grandma. This was probably around the time when my mother was born."

"She's beautiful. Are your mom and your dad still together?"

"No. Well, kind of. They're not technically divorced, but they were separated for a while, after the bust of '97."

The next image when she clicks a controller is of a man sitting in a chair, and behind him are stacks on stacks of pesos and US dollars.

"Oh, this was right before the bust. Look at that smirk on his face! His mustache. He thought he was so cool, so safe, like, 'Nobody will find me!'"

"Have you ever done it?"

"Heroin? No. I took a Percocet once, and I felt like my head was going to roll off my body, so I don't get it. That 'Oh, my life is complete' feeling. Plus I've been around it my whole life. I thought everyone had dads who always had stacks of strange things wrapped tightly, like collectors. To me and my family, 'crime' and 'criminal' and 'illegal' don't exist. I didn't know what my dad was doing was…how do you say…socially unacceptable until I was in high school and all the teachers and students and principals all knew me before I stepped foot in the door, but I didn't know why. I knew my dad's job looked different than my friends' dads', but it was a job. Being on the phone always, the phone always ringing. I wasn't sure who he was talking to, and wasn't curious to know. Like, I felt like if he wanted me to know, he would tell me. Plus he had to make money somehow, so why not make the most? Plus he was always around to take care of us. He made pretty good money always being on the phone at home, I thought."

"What were your friends like in high school? I'm sure you went to a private school, yeah?"

"Well, when I was in elementary school, yes. After the tenth grade, my dad put us in home school because a lot started happening. I couldn't go back to school; it was all too distracting, what my dad was doing. I couldn't focus. It was all over the news. As a little kid, it was worse because I had to always have a guard with me. My dad was always afraid someone would kidnap us and hold us for ransom or bribery or extortion, something like that. He was certain of it. It was less of a headache to hire a guard to watch us 24-7 than it would be to have to pay someone millions in ransom."

She looks at the projector and clicks to an image of a woman she says is her aunt, sitting in a Mercedes Benz with a red bow on it. She said her dad got it for her the day her divorce was finalized because he hated his brother-in-law.

"Was your dad an addict?"

"What's your name again? Sorry."

"Poppy."

"You know, Poppy—that's a pretty name—a lot of high-company dealers and traffickers don't do drugs. They just distribute and sell. To them, like my father, it's strictly business, you know? For instance, say I really liked chocolate cake and was good at making the cakes, and so I opened my own bakery selling my cakes because I liked them so much. But if I were to always eat or become obsessed with my product, I would go out of business."

I stare at her in amazement, thinking of the lunacy that was the poor girl's childhood and how it compared to mine. No wonder she has mental issues. We talk about primary school and how she wasn't allowed to associate with other kids, especially if adults were around. Her dad kept them under close watch at all times, not recognizing the importance of developmental social and communication skills learned from association with peers. When she was a kid, she had a bodyguard, Ronny, with her at all times. He went everywhere she did, except to the bathroom and bed.

In college she felt completely isolated, unable to make any friends because so many people didn't want to be associated with a drug lord's daughter for safety concerns. "It kind of defeated the whole purpose, you know? Like nobody would know who the hell I was if I didn't have some huge black or white dude always three feet behind me. It's the reason I've always had issues with making genuine friends. Most people just want the fame or the story of being 'friends' with a cartel spawn and the glitz and glamour of this secretive world. It's why I love it here. No one is following me around, trying to protect me. Nobody wants anything other than drugs, and I don't think that's too much to ask by today's standards. How many people are in relationships and have friendships where they are selling their souls and bodies or being someone they're not, just to have friends or to not be alone? I think being a traitor to yourself is the worst crime of all, but you don't go to jail for it." I nod, understanding every word.

Most people have partners and friendships out of mutual respect, commonalities of interest, feelings of security, sexual desire, or a commitment to grow toward an ideal. She doesn't understand that some things in life are *supposed* to be free (especially relationships), and instead she was taught that everything costs money, but anyone and anything can be bought.

She tells me the only social interactions she had with her peers were with her brothers and cousins at home. No one outside of the family was ever allowed to come over. Most mothers of middle to high school–age girls didn't approve of a grown male coming over and "watching" the girls, leaving her uninvited to parties and sleepovers.

Next up on screen is a clothing dresser used as a massive jewelry box filled with diamond and gold earrings, crosses, medallions, pearls, loose diamonds, and so on.

"Holy shit," I mumble.

"My mom's jewelry box! When we were little, she would let us wear some and put her heels on and some lipstick, and my sister and I would walk around the house pretending to be her. We idolized her."

"Is she still alive?"

"No. I wish. She had colon cancer and died in 2012."

"Oh, no, I'm sorry. My grandmother died that year too."

"Yeah, when she died, my dad really lost it. Like he would get wasted and walk around the neighborhood with a gun, asking people where she was and shit like that."

"Sounds like a nervous breakdown."

"Yeah, it was, for sure. His murder rate that year, I think he killed, like, twelve people in a day."

"Holy shit, why? Just because of your mom?"

"That and people found out about my mom and just figured he wouldn't be working or moving any weight. When he found out members of a rival gang were trying to take his customers, him, my uncle, and their friend…" She motions slitting her throat.

"Oh my God. Wow."

"Yeah, the kingpins take that shit seriously. Like, that's our livelihood. The Mexican government doesn't do anything for us or get our people jobs, you know, so when you have no help and a lot of land, you grow and sell."

"That's what I hear, sadly. Do you still talk to your dad?"

The screen changes again, with a photo of Ocielle and a friend or relative about her age swinging in a park, enjoying themselves.

"My dad, no. I mean, maybe one day, but not now. He found out I was dating a white guy and flipped. Told me he wanted me out of his house but gave me this house and a million dollars to fix it up, so…I did."

"Well, shit, that's a pretty sweet deal, yeah?"

"Yeah, except I'm screwing a member of the cartel command for heroin and am giving it to my friends. *But* I wanted to show my dad I could be someone without him, you know. Like, he was always—well, one time he told me I would never make it without him, so naturally I was like, yeah, bet me, mothafuckaa."

"When was the last time you talked to him? Do you even want to?"

"Um, I talked to him last, like, a year ago, I think. He's just so busy, you know, trying to maintain the status quo and in and out of prison. He's not exactly stable. He knows where this house is, but he hasn't, like, made any…how do you say…attempt to come out her at all, so whatever." Her bright-red lips have faded away, and the crying has loosened her falsies.

"Do you think he'd be proud of you, or did he want you to run in the opposite direction as him?"

"Nah, he'd be proud, I think. He was a businessman, and I'm a businesswoman; it's simple. I don't need the risk of selling in public places or want people knowing where I come from. This stays between us, okay?" The doorbell rings.

"Yeah, no, I got you," I reassure her. The doorbell rings again.

"Oh, I bet that's Marilyn and the boys. Let's go see! Oh, and you can stay the night if you want. You can tell me about your life and, you know, since you know about mine. We're friends now, right?" she asks, walking down the stairs as I follow.

"Yeah, sure, and thank you!"

"Do you fuck him?"

"Who? Orlando? Nah."

"Oh, why not? Can I?"

"Nah, he's gay. Where has Marilyn been?" I ask, changing the subject.

"Um, I think they went to get money. And pick up my packages."

"You let them borrow your car?" I ask, shocked. "And they come back?"

"What? Yes, of course they come back. Why wouldn't they come back? Like if they steal my car or something?"

"Yeah."

"They won't. They know my cartel would be after them and their families." I don't ask further questions, but it's definitely the single situation where a heroin addict is trusted to bring back a luxury automobile, and on time.

Chapter 24

Jimi

Jimi Phoenix, 24

You really like Kurt because he's a competitive motherfucker like you. He was going to go pro, just like you, but got injured and then on a pain-management plan, just like you. Pain management is pharmaceutical code for "Let's make people think we're *helping* them and making them feel better but really we're just *addicting* them."

In your eyes some of the world's nastiest people seem to work in the medical and pharmaceutical field. You heard that the woman who invented the EpiPen is quadrupling the price or something. Dollar signs, dollar signs, all she sees is dollar signs. Your sister's neighbor's kid actually died because her school was in limbo with the EpiPen controversy and didn't have it one day after school when her best friend unknowingly gave her a praline, leaving her powerless without the pen, and her friend was unable to reach an adult in time. It's also strange how in the great recession of '08, '09, several billion-dollar hospital projects began.

You come from a stable family, just like Kurt, but someone has to be the fuckup in a wealthy family, so that's you. Your brothers and sisters couldn't handle your lack of ambition, they being all laser focused on propelling your dad's tech company while you were more than satisfied working at Walmart. You'd much rather work with normal run-of-the-mill people and deal with a low-stress working environment than try to compete against other tech giants in the area. Fuck them. Fuck the tech boom. This is your family now. They understand you.

OC is an outcast from her wealthy family, like you. She dates white guys; you waste your potential and work at Walmart. Same amount of familial outrage and disapproval. The more they disapproved, the more you withdrew.

You and Kurt are on your way back to the Farm after being OC's bitch boys for the morning and running errands for her. You notice Carlos's car and a red Mercedes that wasn't there when you left.

"Whoa, who's that?" you ask Kurt, trying to figure out who the fine blond chick with the curly hair talking to Prince is. She's wearing jeans that hug her in all the right places with a light-blue hoodie and a bare face. Maybe you two can get sober together and live happily ever after as addiction and drug counselors.

"I dunno. Sure we'll find out soon enough. I'll go give O her stuff or…if Carlos is…here…shit, never mind. Picnic table?" Kurt asks.

"Sure," you say, still curious about the blonde, and hope that's not her boy she just walked outside with. You're starting to feel restless. You get out your hipster fanny pack and remove the last bit of dope you have left with a syringe, a lighter, and some cotton. Time to do a shot for the newest members of Contin Farm.

Chapter 25

Amy

Amy Sintera, 27

You see a young, vibrant duo headed your way, but they are not people you know. Of course, *you* are not who you know anymore. You, Amy, are a shapeless form of who you used to be. Someone's mother, someone's daughter. Now just labeled "the addict." The addict who wants desperately to *want* to quit using, but you just can't get there. You're trapped, powerless, whispering to yourself ambitions for change with a keen inability to follow through, whose tongue wags at the slightest temptation after you said you were done forever, many times.

You study them curiously. These two don't look like junkies, but who even looks like a junkie anymore? Everyone's a junkie. Some people are better at disguises than others. Some wear masks, and some wear masks and simply don't realize it. You dig out your broken mirror in your fanny pack. The only mirror is in Ocielle's room, and the wretched queen usually only permits Marilyn to go in, or whoever else is cleaning her room. You don't much care.

Mirrors seem to be frowned upon here, in this catastrophic, emotionally frozen world you're stuck in. Mirrors now only serve as a luxury for those whose lives have purpose. For people who are going places, doing great things, but not you. In the wilderness of addiction, mirrors are an unfriendly reminder of the condition of your soul, your dull layers of skin, lips parched and disconnected eyes, matching the quality of your moral character. A childless mother, suffering and hollow, more distant than a fading star. You open your fanny pack. You get out your survival tools, sitting on top of a crinkled photo of your son. His happy, smiling face brings tears to your eyes. The yellow outfit, the blue backdrop. The photo was taken eight months before he was taken out of your arms. Looking at him gives you a sudden determination not to give up.

Maybe you will get sober again, see your baby Rokko, and kiss his sweet cheeks. Hold his tiny hand again, if it's even tiny anymore. The same hand that was reaching for you when the paperwork was finalized. Shouldn't the doctors take any blame for this valley of dying stars? After all, they're the ones who supplied the Oxys after Rokko was born. Nothing but a stairway to hell they've set in motion of you getting money, getting dope, getting high. Luckily, Ocielle takes you in, feeds you like a hungry wolf in the forest. You are one of the forgotten addicts of America, but this way you avoid jail, civilians who don't understand you, dirty men who want to take advantage of you, and the father of your child, who claims you are an unfit mother.

Chapter 26

Grave Diagnosis

"There's two over there," responds a man in his midtwenties named Kurt to Orlando and me. Kurt has shoulder-length blond hair and green eyes. He wears a shirt from a skateboarding company and orange board shorts. The ideal beach bum. I ask him whether there are any extra chairs to join him and his friend, who are sitting at a small picnic table covered with spoons, little boxes of Ex-Lax, Pepto-Bismol, lighters, and beer bottles.

We have to go outside since Ocielle kicked everyone out because Carlos is there. Kurt points a half acre away to a few folded lawn chairs on the ground next to a homemade graveyard I hadn't noticed. At least fifteen or so white crosses with writing on them are spread a few feet apart. Some have an assortment of flowers, framed photographs, and stuffed animals.

"Oh my God, are those real graves?" I ask, petrified.

"Yeah, sad but true," Kurt says as he crushes up a soft powder he dumps out of a plastic baggie. I can't keep my eyes off the horrifying sight, pretending that's a normal—and legal—thing to have in a side yard. I ask Orlando to walk over with me.

"This is so fucking illegal. This girl could get life for this. You can't bury someone and not report it."

"How do you know she hasn't?"

"C'mon. She's a heroin dealer. She probably doesn't own this land way out here from the house or pay taxes on it, so anyone with a brain would avoid any government official. Plus she's a cartel offspring! You know they kill their victims and toss them out like rag dolls on the side of the highway or bury them in a ditch, right? This is fucking normal to her!"

"Do you think she killed them or they overdosed?"

"Probably both, but I'd say ODs. Why would she kill them? She has no incentive." We walk and read the crosses. "Rest in Peace, dirrrty Martin-i. You will be missed. We (heart) you. 1989–2015"

The next cross has a pile of dried-up roses and a photo of an attractive redhead with freckles and blue eyes.

"Rest in Peace, Lauren. May you finally find peace. (1997–2014)"

I move down the line, saddened and disturbed.

"Rest in Peace, Baltimore, you Guido motherfucker! (1990–2015)"

"Rest in Paradise, Monica. We will miss you, Pancakes!" (1988–2013)"

"RIP Lauren! We'll watch over Marilyn for you! (1985–2014)"

"Rest in Peace, Jarrod. Take care of Monica for us!" (1987–2014)"

On Jarrod's grave is a framed photo of him and Monica. She looks strangely familiar. The photos of people on the wall inside Casa de la Contin Farm are all people who've passed away, most likely on the grounds.

"Holy shit, these are the people she has on the wall in her house," I say to Orlando, kicking syringes and lids out of the way in disgust.

"What? Oh really? I was wondering who the hell they were. Figured they weren't relatives. This is weird. Let's get the chairs. How much longer do you want to stay for?"

"Um, well, I have an idea I wanna run by you…and since we're friends now, maybe, wouldn't you say?" I ask.

"Sure. I've known you a good five hours now."

"Great! Because friends stick together, so…"

"Oh shit, so what? I'm not doing anything illegal, if that's what you mean."

"No, idiot. My dad actually owns a rehab in Dallas, and I want him to come out here to see this and give these people an intervention."

"You've got to be kidding. That's the reason you wanted to come out here so bad, right? It all makes sense now. Was wondering why someone who wasn't an addict would wanna spend time with junkies if they didn't have to."

"Geez, Orlando, be an asshole, will you? Just because they're dope fiends doesn't mean they're not humans who deserve respect."

"Sure. I mean, they are humans; you're right. But I guess when you lose a twin sibling to addiction, it sort of leaves a bitter taste in your mouth, especially toward others who still have a chance. Plus now that I think about it, they're more like zombies than humans." We start walking back to the others.

"Kind of, I mean—"

"Think about it. You get high, you zone out or pass out, and then right when the high wears off, you're on the prowl again for more. It's never enough. You're laser focused on one thing and one thing only. Get high, come down, get more, repeat. Over and over and over again."

When Orlando gets passionate, he (humorously) talks with his hands. When people talk with their hands, they're really trying to sell you on their ideas. It reminds me of my parents when I get lectured on anything ranging from going twenty-five over to smoking pot with my friends or wiring money to someone from Craigslist who said he needed a tutor for his son who was coming to America and wanted to pay me fifty dollars an hour.

"Some sad shit over there, yeah?" asks Kurt, firing the underbelly of a spoon. While watching the bubbly tar melt, his eyes are yellow, still, and blank, revealing a damaged body and soul who is cutting himself off more and more from his innermost self and real happiness as the liquid gets hotter.

"They were all heroin addicts?" I ask, sitting in a chair Orlando opens for me.

"Yep. Lived here at the Farm for a while. Some were here for a while, others as little as a few weeks…if that, maybe"

"What about cops? They haven't wandered over with questions about the crosses or the littering? Obviously someone has to be living here," says Orlando, taking a sip of his beer.

"Don't have 'em. In a city with less than two thousand people, we don't need cops. Taxpayers won't do it."

"Wait, y'all don't have police out here?" I ask, at first excited and then horrified at the thought.

"Umm…I think we did, like, in the eighties, but there weren't enough people living here to pay 'em. Hand me that belt, bro," says Kurt to Jimi, who is lighting a cigarette.

"I'm Jimi, by the way," Jimi says to Orlando and me, barely able to open his eyes, let alone shake our hands. Kurt unzips his purple fanny pack and gets out a needle. The fanny pack system is apparently the way to go here. Everyone seems to have one except Ocielle. They contain everything a heroin addict needs, including but not limited to syringes, cotton, spoons, lighters, cigarettes, and bags of dope. Kurt wraps a beat-up leather belt around his bicep, bites off an orange lid from a syringe, and spits it on the ground. He pulls his new, warm concoction into the needle.

He slaps a vein in his elbow and says, "Get ready, boys. It's snack time." He shuffles the syringe into his vein after a brief struggle, sending the brown butter into his body. When I see the blood retracting back into the syringe, I can feel it. The anxious rush as if someone just pushed me out of a ten-story window. Dammit.

I sit still, breathing deep, afraid of what I might do or say in the midst of an attack, since in the past I've asked complete strangers for drugs. I wonder whether I even introduced myself first or just went for it. I'll never know.

Hopefully, Orlando will protect me and not let me do a shot of heroin if I ask for it.

"Hey, get me my purse, please."

"Another one?" he asks. I probably nod. Jimi is watching me curiously as Kurt slowly removes the needle and lets out a deep "Fuuuccckkk," then smiles like a little kid on

Christmas morning.

"Can you get me a water? Do y'all have water here?" I ask, idiotically, but it feels right at the time.

"In the house. I can grab you one," says Jimi.

"I'll give you a Valium for some!" I tell him excitedly. My toes burn. Everyone and everything are fading away, and I can't hear anything; I'm able to concentrate only on what is going on internally. If I stay with it, I like to believe, I have a better watch over it. Less chance I'll have of passing out, throwing up, peeing on myself, having a heart attack, and so on.

"I hate this shit," I say.

"I know, you tell me that every time. Here's your Valium," Orlando says. My eyes have glazed over. I am no longer present. I am held captive to my brain. In these moments I understand why people use if they have whatever funky shit I do. It takes control, like visits from the devil.

My arm starts to bend. I take Orlando's beer and pour some on my feet because my toes are on fire. He probably doesn't appreciate it. I would like to have seen his reaction. Waves, my brain is going for a swim. Will I come back to shore this time? Each time feels as if I won't. Here we go, upside down, around this roller coaster, now it's bumpy, we're crashing. Go! Swim back to shore in my skull and be Poppy again, please. I'm over this.

I look at Kurt, who's nodding out and hunched with posture of a ninety-year-old woman with osteoporosis. I can hear Orlando say something to Kurt but can't figure out what; it's all muffled. My throat is dry. Water would help.

"Here you go," says Jimi, handing me a chilled bottle of Ozarka.

"Hell yeah, thank you so much!" My brain is back. I can see, feel, think—same old Poppy. Now is the fun part. All the guys at the table are beautiful, especially Orlando…and Jimi. Don't love Orlando, Poppy. He has baggage. But I like kids.

Maybe it's not baggage. We couldn't have gotten luckier with the weather out here in West Texas. Nothing in the blue sky except plane exhaust, crossing other pilots' steps. This is paradise.

"Is he okay?" I ask, pointing to Kurt.

"Are…*you*…okay?" Jimi asks, more concerned I am having some sort of out-of-body experience sober than Kurt is after a shot of tar. I look at my hand and the bottle that came out of nowhere.

"Wait…dammit, who brought me water?" I ask, disappointed and embarrassed. Kurt and Jimi probably think I'm nuttier and worse off than they are out here in the middle of nowhere, working for a socially inept but insanely wealthy Latina. "Oh, no. What did I say?"

"You said you'd give me a Valium?"

I look at Orlando for clarification.

"Yep, you did! And you poured *my* beer on *your* feet."

I laugh and wiggle my toes, noticing they're damp and sticking to my flip-flop. "Sorry. Why'd I do that? That's a first."

"You said your feet were burning."

"You still want a Valium?" I ask Jimi.

"Yeah. I mean…Valium won't do shit for me, but hey, you never know."

I reach into my bag and give him what I promised. The blond chick who was nodding off at the dinner table comes outside and looks around. She walks slowly to the graveyard and stands in front of Lauren's cross. Flowers slip out of her hand, and she collapses on top of the grave in agony, burying her head in her hands. Kurt tells us about Lauren, her close friend who died last week.

"You chase the high until you're dead. There's nothing left. Doctors fucked us over, and this is what we have become," says Jimi.

"What do you mean, doctors fucked y'all over? You got the prescription; you put too many in your body; you got addicted. Physicians do tend to set the ball in motion, but you ultimately have the control over your life, not them," I remind Jimi.

"A fast injury and a sixty-dayer of Amy's, and a year later here I am. It escalates quickly, you know? Taking more…and needing more, then it becomes…too expensive to handle then…and a buddy…of mine asked…if I tried heroin because…it could save me a lot of cash." Kurt keeps on. "Jimi here was injured boarding…Marilyn got hooked on plastic surgery and the pills, so there she is…I think Prince originally broke his foot and got on pills, got addicted, then soon started throwing himself down flights of stairs *just to get morphine.*"

"Not Prince! Isn't an addict," says Kurt.

"Yeah, Prince. True. Prince doesn't think he's a real addict, because he snorts H instead of injecting it. Says IV use is for corrupt, homeless street junkies. Thinks he's more dignified and shit 'cause he shoves it with his boogers."

"So he thinks he's not really an addict because he doesn't inject?" I ask, smiling at the popular misconception surrounding addiction.

"Nope," says Kurt, "definitely the denial addict that tells themselves anything to avoid being a junkie. The type that still believes if a doctor prescribes it, then it must be safe."

Jimi says, "It must be safe" with Kurt, as you say "Amen" after a prayer, almost chanting the cliché they've heard a million times. Thousands, if not millions, of people all over the world still maintain this false belief.

"I heard…somebody…say once that…the opioid…epidemic in the United States is a product of terrorism," says Jimi.

"What? No way," says Orlando.

"Yeah, man, it kind of…makes…sense if you think…about it. It's a pathetic way to get…Americans to…kill…their own people."

"How'd you get here, again, Jimi? I know…you told me, but I may have been high," says Kurt, smiling and unzipping his fanny pack.

"Boarding accident in Rio. Broke my collarbone."

"And a doctor gave you…" I ask. Kurt and Orlando light a cigarette.

"Fentanyl patches…and those suckers too, those yummy bastards."

"Aww, bro, you got those suckers? Lucky," Kurt says.

"Fentanyl seems a little harsh for a broken collarbone, no? Only terminal patients should have access to fentanyl," I say.

"Yeah. But it's what I was…given, so…you can't…blame…the…injured."

"Well, yeah, you can, though. It's not the doctor's fault if you notice there's a problem and don't really care to fix it. Like if a doctor gives you a medication you didn't know you were allergic to, but you keep taking it, well—"

"What's she's trying to say is, at some point you need to take responsibility for your actions," says Orlando. "What do they say in Texas? Pull yourself up by your bootstraps and deal with it? Put your big-girl panties on?" he asks, looking at me.

"Yeah, something like that," I say, trying not to laugh in such a desperate situation.

"Yeah, well, that's a lot easier…to say…than…" says Jimi, slowly leaning forward.

When someone is high on heroin, it's like witnessing someone who has been shot in the stomach in slow motion, minus the blood. The body collapses into a ball as a primal defense instinct, sensing it's in grave danger and needs to be as small as possible to retain energy and ward off predators. The mouth stays wide open as the respiratory system slows, trying to capture as much air as possible to avoid shutting down completely. The spine can no longer hold itself together, and like moving through mud, the addict slowly falls forward, melting into the earth. Similar to insects when they're sprayed with Raid. They don't die instantly. They instead will try to escape from the poison, but a minute or so later, it encapsulates them, and having used all their energy trying to escape, they are overcome. They pull their limbs in and die.

Kurt's face has a grimace on it; he's not seeming to enjoy the high at all but is more like a pale and struggling cockroach who has just sprayed himself with Raid.

The wind stirs the Ex-Lax boxes and cigarette butts in an eerie circle next to our table.

"Do y'all have an ashtray or…" asks Orlando, stamping his cigarette butt out on the table.

"Yeah, dude. Somewhere. I think it's Janis's turn to have…cleaned them," says Jimi, before continuing. "Kurt here, he's from Boston. The typical…northeastern male junkie. They give out pills…like they're going out of…style up…there."

"Yeah, real talk. Fuck Boston…those docs are fucking assholes. Like, 'Here's a sixty-dayer, but don't come back for more, even though you're addicted and need more not to literally feel like you're dying.' I mean, shit…just had a migraine for, like…a month, bro, and a doctor gave me Oxys when I was nineteen…for a migraine…of course you, like, trust 'em, you know. Like, those are educated motherfuckers. They're not going to give you something that's, like, unsafe, ya know? With their Harvard educations and residencies and shit."

"Whatever keeps you coming back," says Orlando.

"Ya, for real. I tell…ya, once…I had my first Oxy hit…I was in fucking heaven, bro, real talk. I had found my missing piece to my life, y'know? No more headaches, ever, unless…I am withdrawing, but that's a whole other animal to deal with…as an addict."

"Did you live with your parents at the time? How did they not know how crazy opiates are? A doctor issued opiates to a kid for migraines?"

"Yeah, they knew I went to the doctor but, like, nothing about opiates. They just assumed whatever a doc gave me would be safe"—this time Jimi says it with him—"and helpful, like it should be."

"Scary world when you can't trust doctors," I say.

"How about you? How long have you been on Valium?" Jimi asks.

"About a week. Doctor gave me them for the panic episodes like you saw. One even gave me hydrocodone since I mentioned they gave me headaches, and Klonopin and Valium."

"Panic episodes? You need Valium 'cause you're anxious? Like I needed Oxys just because I have a headache."

I ignore Jimi's remark, though he has a point.

"You don't remember what you say, right?" Kurt asks, suddenly curious. "You're hand curls, and you say it feels like your brain is floating?"

"Yep!"

"No, that doesn't sound like a panic attack to me, bro. That sounds like a seizure, real talk."

"What? A seizure? No, I'm not...epileptic."

"Yeah, dude, you...might be. My cousin had the same thing, except he would have more spasms...but he said his brain would go through the same shit. Literally...just...like you said. He would...say his feet burned, and I'm like, what, bro? It's forty degrees out. Then he wouldn't remember it. I think he actually went to Australia to have brain surgery or something." I listen with my mouth open as I did when first seeing the North Tower getting struck by an airplane in 2001. Am I really having seizures?

"Oh my God! You think? What else did he do?" I ask, demanding to know more.

"Um, he would, like...his eye would twitch like yours did, and he would say the weird stuff. Sometimes he'd get naked. Said he felt like his clothes were on fire."

For the next half hour, Kurt tells me everything he knows about his cousin and his epilepsy, how he had a scar on his brain from birth and that's what caused him to have seizures. His cousin wasn't allowed to drive or take baths for safety reasons. Even though Kurt was high as a kite, and although he probably wouldn't remember our conversation, I would never forget it.

Chapter 27

Janis

Janis Bresken, 28

It looks like two new people are moving in, but they…don't get high? You're not sure as you walk outside with Amy. Your leg is still sore and disgusting. You live for winters so you can wear pants, but Texas in May can be brutal in jeans, so you're stuck with shorts. It was good stuff, eats the flesh off your body. That's how you know it's good.

Like when someone overdoses, all the junkies in town want to know who the person bought the dope from, not so they can kill them but so they can score. Luckily, you got away from it in time. You know people in Baltimore who are basically paralyzed from it. They can't hold down food; it eats their insides out. It's cannibalism in liquid form.

You were always a straight-A student, voted "Most Likely to Succeed" and prom queen your senior year of high school. If they could see you now. No, you definitely don't want that.

No one would want to know their UHHS senior prom queen is now a junkie with an eating disorder and a molding leg who's been exposed to a flesh-and-organ-eating brand of junk called desomorphine, containing red phosphorus and paint thinner, who inserted it into her own body, creating her own nightmare. You shoot at your own risk; you got what you deserved. You just want to feel numb.

After being an addict for six years krokodil was the one thing that would for *sure* get you high, as all the other resources for out-of-body experiences no longer enough. One thing you know for sure: very few people here are even getting high anymore. They are only maintaining, which is pretty easy to do when you live with a cartel spawn with endless amounts of dope.

Ocielle doesn't even get high. She wouldn't understand, but at least she prevents everyone from getting sick, even if it kills you. It won't kill you, though. You come from a family of war veterans, body builders, and cage fighters, and that's just your father's side. Your mother's side has survived genocides.

You someday want to go back home but don't want to deal with the street life. Just another junkie crawling up a corner, looking for work. Your parents won't let you live with them anymore, since you pawn "everything you see," and when they came back from the Bahamas that one time and their jewelry was gone, so were you. It's nice living here, where you don't have to tell anyone any lies. You're being honest now, and getting smack an honest way: through hard work for Ocielle.

Chapter 28

Dinner

In the kitchen Ocielle digs through the freezer for turkey meatballs to go with the spaghetti dinner. Since she has written off her family and vice versa, she's adamant about the Contin Farm campers eating together on Sundays. She charges a quarter of a gram of smack if they want to eat, which includes all you can eat and drink.

If you don't drink beer, wine, or tequila, you are having water. Growing up, Ocielle was always watching her family chef, Mona, in the kitchen, telling herself one day she would cook for her family with the skills she learned from Mona, and she has.

Since her father was always on the phone and her mother would be out shopping or watching Mexican soap operas, Mona taught little Ocielle how to prepare all types of Mexican cuisines, plus an assortment of Italian, Greek, Ethiopian, Vietnamese, and French cuisines. When she yells out a terrifyingly loud "DINNERTIME," once outside and once inside, Prince comes downstairs from the arcade room, and Orlando, Amy, Kurt, Jimi, Janis, Marilyn, and I come in from outside.

"I'm starving. Does she take cash?" Orlando asks Jimi on the way in.

"That's a good question," Jimi says slowly. "I'm gonna go with…yes."

The addicted don't walk at a feverish pace with their heads high and shoulders back. The residents at Contin Farm walk with their heads down in shame. Orlando and I breeze past them all at a normal pace, arriving to the kitchen first.

"Hey, do you mind if we stay for dinner?" I ask Ocielle. "I have some cash." Her brown puppy-dog eyes light up.

"Nah, it's okay. Y'all are my guests tonight." She winks as she retrieves garlic bread from the oven, spreading a scent of food porn.

"Oh, thank you," says Orlando. It is the first time I've seen him smile since we've been here. He's seemingly spending all his time in the arcade, playing Pac-Man, air hockey, or foosball with Prince or whomever else.

"Yeah, it looks delicious!"

"Thanks. My family's chef taught me all the good stuff. Plus it's nice to have sober people around, you know? Makes you not feel like the crazy one." In that moment I pity her. Her makeup is smudged from her entertaining romp with Carlos.

"Hey, what are we having? Spring rolls?" asks Prince. "Hey, how y'all doin'?" he asks Orlando and me. He has changed for dinner, now wearing a suit jacket and tie.

"Hey, Prince! We're good, just chatting with Ocielle, who so kindly offered to have us as guests for dinner."

"Oh…well, isn't that nice?" He smiles. The door opens, and we can hear Marilyn bickering with Jimi about the LA Dodgers when Kurt chimes in and shuts the whole conversation down. Janis walks in with Amy.

"Oh, wow, incredible though it smells of delicious things," says Amy, taking a huge inhale. They all line up around the marble kitchen island and dig through their fanny packs to get the quarter ounces to pay for their dinners. Orlando and I watch in fascination as this daily ritual unfolds. Ocielle has a scale waiting by the stove, and while everyone gets his or her method of payment ready, she serves us first, a heaping plate of spaghetti, turkey meatballs with marinara sauce, and a thick slice of still-steaming garlic bread.

"Thank you so much. This looks delicious," I say.

"You're welcome. We have tequila, beer, wine. Take whatever you'd like. Help yourselves."

I assure her I'm great with water and sit down at the dining table, which seats twenty-five, with Orlando right behind me.

I turn and watch everyone in line with fascination while Orlando stuffs his face. Kurt hands Ocielle a tiny baggie of dope. She weighs it and says, "Okay, you're good to go," and serves him. When Jimi gets his supply out, she weighs it. "Nope, more. Don't try to play."

Prince asks her to put his dinner only on the left side of his plate. Ocielle rolls her eyes but obeys.

"How much do you want? Are you going to actually eat it?" Ocielle asks Janis, who's next in line.

"Oh, yeah, Ocielle. I fucking love your spaghetti. You…know this."

"And you'll eat it? No throwing up after, okay? None of that spitting it into your napkin crap either. Okay?"

Janis forces a smile and a nod, then turns around to flip her off. It's interesting how eating dinner reveals so much about people. In mere minutes I've learned that the upbeat and collected Prince struggles with obsessive-compulsive disorder and Janis has bulimia or anorexia or both.

After Marilyn gets her meal and everyone is seated, we're told that Prince always says grace before anyone eats. We bow our heads.

"Dear Heavenly Father, we…thank…you…for the nourishment…this food will bring to our bodies and souls, and to Ocielle…for…feeding us…mangy…dope…fiends. Oh, and thank you…for our…guests…and…Carlos…and…Mexico. Amen."

Everyone repeats, "Amen."

"Do y'all eat lunch here together too every day?" I ask as everyone except Janis and Marilyn eats spaghetti. Janis and Marilyn are moving it around on their plates, talking about how good it looks but not yet eating. Marilyn cuts all hers up and separates the spaghetti from the meatballs. Janis does the same, except she puts the whole meatball into her mouth, licking off all the sauce before pulling it back out.

"Nah, really just dinner is all we eat. Sometimes, if the dope's good enough, it'll…make…you nauseous, so we usually just stick to one meal a day," says Jimi, taking a sip of his Chardonnay.

I hadn't noticed Janis's boney structure until dinner, but her collar and chest bones are clearly defined, and she leans forward to take a bite, her thin skin having to stretch to cover the well-defined bones. I glance at Orlando, who's finished with his food and notices Janis's chest also. Janis, Kurt, Jimi, Marilyn, Prince, and Amy are all commenting on the deliciousness of the food around the table, saying it is the best they've had in a while and how great of a cook Ocielle is. The approval makes her glow. Janis puts a single noodle in her mouth, chews painfully slowly, and then swallows. Marilyn licks the sauce off the noodles and meatballs, leaving a collection of separated al dente pasta and chopped-up meatballs.

"You need to eat more," says Ocielle to Janis and Marilyn. The looks on their faces go from satisfied to horrified.

"Dude. My stomach though," says Marilyn in a soft voice, putting her fork down and looking at the ends of her hair. "I need a trim. Where's the nearest salon? My ends look like a powerless inmate's doing life in prison. Without parole."

"The backyard," says Jimi. "Ocielle did mine last week. Only charges a quarter ounce."

"Whaaat, for a trim, O? Did you even go to cosmo school?"

"No. I went to life school. The school of life. It's free. Now finish eating. You're just constipated. Eat anyway," Ocielle says with her mouth full. I notice deep white scars on both of Marilyn's arms and wrists I hadn't seen before.

"By the way, you know I love y'all, but who keeps littering in the front? Those stupid orange caps? Like, that's a dead fucking giveaway. Does someone here *want* the cops to come?"

Orlando looks around as if he wants to shout, "PREACH!"

The spaghetti-and-heroin mix must have really done everyone in, as no one is interested in Ocielle's complaints.

"Whatever. Whoever brings me the most trash gets back their quarter."

"Do you still want us to do the toilets and vacuum too, like we usually do after dinner?" asks Jimi.

Kurt, Amy, and Prince pull their heads back up, suddenly interested in her offer.

"Not tonight, unless you need dope. Who's out?" Ocielle asks the table.

Jimi and Prince raise their hands.

"Well, then y'all can clean the toilets and vacuum. Also I have dirty laundry in my room. If everyone else here wants a place to stay tonight, y'all need to pick up all of your shit outside, or everyone is sleeping outside."

"Yeah, right," says Kurt, the only one not afraid to stand up to Ocielle.

"Wanna bet, fucker? I have sleeping bags!"

Kurt rolls his eyes. He and Jimi get up, taking their plates into the kitchen. Everyone else follows their lead, leaving Orlando, Ocielle, and me.

"Addicts are such slobs," says Ocielle.

"Yeah, they sure can be. But hey, would it be all right if Orlando and I stay the night tonight? I have an obsession with teepees. I figured if you didn't mind?"

"You have an obsession with teepees or Orlando?" she asks me, smiling. "Yeah, that should be fine. Y'all can take the teepee in the backyard again. Can you two clean in the morning? Or at least wash the sheets?"

"Um, sure."

I'm sure Orlando and I are wearing out our welcome, and quickly, but I'm on a mission. We have to act like one of the campers—only sober—until my dad gets there.

I go into the kitchen to help Ocielle with the dishes.

"You got this, yeah? *The Bachelor*'s on tonight, and I'm way behind on *Judge Judy*. Yesterday's episode reminded me of a case I dealt with years ago, when the plaintiff was too high to testify. Case got thrown out, that moron." I roll my eyes but humor her.

"Um, sure, yeah, that's fine. I'll clean." Ocielle flees, leaving me alone with a pile of dirty dishes and marinara-splashed countertops. I haven't washed any of my clothing from the initial trip and am getting tired of my sweatshirt-and-jeans attire. I grab my clothes and throw them in the wash.

Ocielle comes back a few minutes later, looking for Twizzlers and beer.

"Where the fuck? Someone better not have eaten them!" I change the subject before she gets too angry. Still searching for candy, she opens a can of Tecate and randomly reveals she has a thing for Jimi.

"Really, Ocielle? He's a drug addict. You of all people should know—"

"I know, I know, but he's so fine, though, right?"

"I mean, he's a cute kid, but he…has his demons."

"Who doesn't though, ya know? Think about it. No one, girl." I realize I'm now speaking with Shirley, the more illogical partier out of the three that I know of.

"Umm, not too many people have demons they need to shoot up over. I mean, there's a few."

"Yeah, I know, but I feel like I could *save* him. Like I could ask him if he wanted to go to rehab, and I'd pay for it. I know a bunch of people who've gotten clean, and they're the best people I know now."

I stay quiet, rubbing the grease and sauce off the cookie sheets.

"Don't you think that's a good idea? Aren't you sober?" she asks.

"Do I think what's a good idea? You dating an active-and-loving-it user? Absolutely not. I wouldn't want that for anyone."

"I mean, Pop-pee—ha! PAPI!" she says loudly, laughing. "I mean, I can ask him if he wants to go to rehab. Then maybe he'll say yes, and we live happily ever after!"

"No. No. No, Ocielle. Okay. No. I mean, if he wants to get sober, then by all means, give this conversation a few days; then ask him when he's alone and or feeling vulnerable. But you'd have to be willing to send him, and he needs to actually *want* to go. But you don't ask someone to go to treatment like you'd ask a neighbor if you can borrow a cup of sugar. 'Hey, listen. I think you're fine and you should be sober, so will you go to rehab for me?' It doesn't work like that."

Ocielle makes a strange, confused face, like a toddler who just dropped her ice cream on the ground. She grabs her Twizzlers and heads back upstairs.

While I'm loading the dishes, Marilyn comes in quietly.

"Where's Ocielle?" she whispers.

"Um, upstairs, I think," I whisper back. Stumbling and struggling to stay on her feet, she heads into the pantry. Her hollow eyes are sunken in, from not only heroin but also her lack of food. Her skin is blotchy and consistent with drug abuse. In the small bedroom-size pantry, Marilyn looks at her options. She grabs a bag of Lay's potato chips and shoves ten or so into her mouth. After the chips come the s'mores-flavored Pop-Tarts. I hear her moaning with pleasure every time she takes a bite. She opens another package of something while I start sweeping.

"Still hungry?"

"Yeah, starving. I wait until O goes to bed and come in here and tear up the pantry."

"Why don't you eat your whole dinner or…"

"Because…they're carbs," she says, chewing her Pop-Tart, and smiles. "Usually I'll chew and spit, but she was watching me at dinner, so I just didn't eat much. She can't force it down my throat." She grabs a container of animal crackers and scoops out a handful. Silver Pop-Tart wrappers and Cheetos sit on the floor. "Want some?"

"No, thanks, I just ate. And I'm cleaning."

"Sorry, don't worry. I'll pick it up when I'm done. Is there ice cream?" she asks with wide eyes, almost pushing me over to get to the freezer. "Oh, fuck yeah!" she whispers. She grabs a spoon and parades around kitchen with the Häagen-Dazs, tells me how good it is, while I clean.

I turn on the dishwasher, and Marilyn trashes the pint of ice cream, grabs a couple of wrappers and chips from the floor, and throws them away.

"Okay, um, have a good night," says Marilyn in her raspy voice.

"You too." She disappears, and I grab my things from the house to take to the teepee. On my way out, I hear someone violently puking in the bathroom.

Chapter 29

Teepee Action

I walk outside to the teepee, exhausted and smelling like garlic bread. The sky is the largest I've seen, glittering with stars, revealing constellations I've only read about but never witnessed. Perfectly clear and aligned—you feel God's presence in an overhaul of beauty like the one above. I stand and stare in awe, waiting for a unicorn—or the equivalent—to gallop through, pure magic in all directions. Orlando is lying on a mattress on the ground, reading a book.

"Where'd you get that? And have you seen the sky?"

"Um, library. Yeah, it's pretty, right? Where've you been?"

"Cleaning that massive goddamn kitchen. Ocielle wants to sober up Jimi and date him."

"Ha! Good luck with that one, lady." Orlando yawns and stands up. "Yeah, she's nuts. Probably the nuttiest of all," he says, pulling his T-shirt over his head, messing up his thick hair. I try not to look, but the privacy in a teepee is limited. He has a tattoo of something on his chest.

"And Marilyn is a bulimic. Raided the pantry and barfed it up."

"God. How lovely."

"What's that on your chest?" I ask.

"Um, that's called a tattoo," he says, grinning.

"Oh, I've never seen one so fucked up. I wasn't sure if it was a tattoo or…if you got into a fight with a paintball gun." I remove my earrings, awaiting his response.

"You know what?"

"What?"

"Fuck you," he says, stepping over to me, and he grabs my face, kissing me. I am caught completely off guard. His tongue dances with mine, tasting like cigarettes and Sprite. He slips his hands up my back, unfastening my bra quicker than any man has before. I slip my hands into the back pockets of his jeans, remembering him flipping them out earlier when he wanted a ride. I smile, midpassion, and he gently pulls away.

"What are you smiling about?" he asks, studying my face.

"Oh, just…nothing. What are you smiling at?" I ask, gently biting his bottom lip before he has time to answer.

"Oh, just nothing…wanting to do this all damn day, is all."

"Um, do what?"

"Funny."

Later that night I'm woken up by my toes being touched by something moist and rough. Initially I giggle, thinking it is a dream, but I flutter my tired eyes open to see what it is. I freeze when I see a monstrous bobcat with blue eyes looking at me.

"Oh my God!" I whisper, powerless and unsure of what to do. Should I scream? Play dead? I look at Orlando, who is (of course) asleep.

"Orlando!" I whisper, afraid to make any sudden moves or speak too loudly, desperately hoping he will wake up and know what to do. He just grunts and flips over, offering no assistance. The cat looks at me, then Orlando, and then back at me. My life is over. I will be devoured by a bobcat in the West Texas desert on a heroin farm under a pretty night sky.

Orlando rolls over and yells, "What, fuckers?" in his sleep. The startled cat darts off.

"Oh my, thank God! The lion! There was a fucking lion, Orlando!"

"Whaaaat? Where? Lions don't live here, Poppy."

I say, hysterical, "Well, I dunno what the fuck it was, Orlando! But it was a huge bobcat or mountain lion!"

He is more concerned with getting rest than trying to stay alive. "Okay, Poppy. Well, it's gone now, so go on back to sleep," he says, patting me on the leg. My heart is racing.

"Are you serious! I was literally planning on what I was going to be wearing at my funeral in my head!"

"Okay! Good night!" he says.

If I had my phone, I would be Googling about how many desert bobcat / mountain lions slay humans in their sleep a year.

Chapter 30

Morning Routine

The next morning I'm prematurely woken by the sounds of a vacuum. I peep out of the teepee and see Amy's bed-headed self vacuuming with the windows open. The sun hasn't risen but is staining the dark-blue sky with orange. Orlando's still asleep. I go inside to get coffee, or at least find a way to make it myself. Jimi is in his pj's, washing dishes with no shirt on; an array of random tattoos covers his chest, and his fanny pack wraps around his waist.

"Hey, good morning," he says, rinsing off a plate. He's unusually chipper in the morning, much more energetic than I've seen him before. He is almost an average American who just ate breakfast, drank some coffee, and is now getting ready to go about his day, catching a matinee with his lover, returning work calls or e-mails, going to the gym, or going to Lowe's to get a box for composting or a weed whacker.

"Good morning!"

"There's coffee in there." He motions with his head to the cabinet since his hands are full.

"Cool, thanks."

"Excuse me. Good morning to ya!" says Prince with a mop and an empty bucket.

"You doin' the mopping?" asks Kurt, coming from upstairs. He too is topless and in boxers, sporting a Superman fanny pack.

"Yeah."

"Fuck, what's left then?" asks Kurt.

"You need to make Ocielle breakfast or give her a massage. Everything else has been done. Amy's vacuuming."

"Kurt, come here!" Ocielle yells.

Kurt rolls his eyes and goes upstairs. He opens Ocielle's bedroom door to find her in her bra sitting up in bed, fresh faced. Her long, thick black hair blankets her shoulders and size E chest.

"Hey. So Amy's vacuuming, Jimi's doing the kitchen, Prince is mopping, and Marilyn's doing toilets. Since you're the last one up, you need to…let's see. I want breakfast, so you can make me breakfast, change the oil in my car, or give me a full-body massage for an hour, or…eat me."

"How much?"

"For what?"

"Breakfast."

Ocielle rolls her eyes, disappointed at Kurt's response. "A fold."

"Fine. What do you want for breakfast?"

"Scrambled eggs and two pancakes with agave nectar and a papaya with seasoning."

It is like a well-oiled machine. Everyone needs a morning fix, so they start the day cleaning or running errands. A chart on the wall documents who does what. Kurt comes back downstairs, his fanny pack jingling, and I sit at a bar stool and sip my coffee.

"What'd she say?" asks Jimi, snickering.

"I could change her oil, make her breakfast, eat her out, or give her a massage."

"For how much?"

"A fucking fold, bro. I mean, shit, I'm the one who needs the massage. My legs are fucking killing me."

"What? A fold for an hour massage?" Jimi smiles as he wipes down the countertops. Kurt grabs a skillet.

"Yeah, I know, right? Like fuck you. Of course I'm going to do what takes the *least* amount of time, you know, so I'm like, breakfast it is!" Kurt sneezes. "Aw, shit, I'm starting to get sick. Dammit." His forehead starts to bead with sweat. He's getting not sick in the normal sense but dope sick.

"Hey," Orlando says, strolling in from outside. He rubs his eyes with his palms. He looks cute in the morning. "You makin' eggs, bro?"

"Yeah, for Ocielle. You want some?"

"Yeah, sure, thanks."

"Well, you can make some after I get Princess her breakfast and get me my dope."

"Hey! When the chores are done, who wants to go swimming? Poppy and Orlando, y'all can come too!" Ocielle yells from upstairs. I forgot there's an indoor pool, absentmindedly passing by the metal door you need a code to open.

Orlando and I look at each other.

"We don't have bathing suits!" I yell back.

"That's okay, Poppy. I have a Gucci you can borrow, and Orlando, I'm sure Kurt has one you can wear. Or Carlos might have left one here. I'll check and see."

"There's a pool?" asks Orlando.

"Yeah. You know that metal door through the bedroom? It leads to it," Kurt says.

I know I shouldn't drink coffee. I usually try to stay away from caffeine since it can trigger my episodes, especially if I'm doing something exciting or around a lot of people or stimulation. The mixture earlier of the loud vacuuming, the washing, the smell of eggs cooking, the warmth of my coffee, and the thought of swimming all replay in my mind, and my eyes glaze over. Here we go. Just sit still. Don't say anything. This means that stupid bipolar medication isn't working. I think about my panic attacks actually being seizures, and that makes me sink deeper. I take deep breaths and clasp my hands together as tightly as I can, trying not to be carried away. I can feel my eyelid twitching. Here's the deep part. I feel as if everyone and the kitchen were falling into a hole. I have visions of being on a pirate ship in rocky waters, and Prince, Kurt, Jimi, Orlando, Marilyn, and Amy are all on board. I remember that Orlando and I slept together last night. I see the mountain lion's face. The dog at the Shell. The Dalmatian. I'm hoping nobody is talking to me or expecting a reaction. I am in a different universe and will be gone for a couple of minutes only, I hope.

Long, painful seconds pass, but then I feel it lifting, thank God. I'm coming back up for air and won't drown, suffocate, or be someone else. My brain feels cleaned and sanitized, like dishes coming out of a piping-hot dishwasher. I'm suddenly thrilled to be surrounded by such amazing people who have great potential. I can help them.

"Kurt, have you slept with Ocielle?" I powerlessly ask, adding that I also need water.

He flips the cakes over and slides them on the plate next to the eggs.

"Let me answer your question after I get high," he says and takes the full plate upstairs. It is weird. He didn't react as though it was the totally random and inappropriate question that it was, but I'm humiliated when Orlando later tells me about it. He starts cooking eggs, which he doesn't know will be mine. We eat our breakfast outside by the teepee since it's nice out, probably seventy-five degrees. I want to act cool, but I also want to know how he feels about last night. Do I bring it up or pretend it never happened?

Since we slept together, I can't help but feel emotionally involved now, but then again, he lives in Tucson and I in Dallas. It could never work out anyway, so why not just declare him a good time and carry on?

"You wanna go swimming?" I ask, looking out at the acreage of auburn earth with random scatterings of miniature bushes and loads of white pebbles.

"Shit, I dunno. Did you call your parents? When are they supposed to be here?"

"Yeah, yesterday. They said they're going to try to be here by tonight, but who knows. Why do you hate it here so much, anyway? This view is not something you see every day."

"Yeah, you forget I'm from Tucson."

"Well, whatever. Just suck it up, okay? You get to go swimming. Think of it as a vacation."

"Oh, for sure. Sleeping in a teepee and being surrounded by heroin addicts in the weirdest situation I've ever been in in my life doesn't qualify as a vacation, lady."

"Y'all wanna swim?" asks Ocielle, coming outside in purple python triangle bikini from the nineties.

"I do. I dunno about Orlando. What the fuck else are you going to *do*, Orlando?" I ask.

"Well, since your dad texted me last night and told me he'd pay me a grand to babysit you until he got here, it looks like I'm going swimming," he whispers, inaudible to Ocielle. My mouth falls open.

"Yeah, he's going," I say, smiling. "He just loves to swim," I yell, winking at him. I follow Ocielle to her room, where she has her Gucci bikini from two whole seasons ago, and it's basically useless. I look at the size of Ocielle's chest compared to mine, concerned.

"Ummm…"

"Here you go. It's adjustable," she says, handing the bikini to me.

Ocielle and I hear a loud thump coming from the dining room. She drops the swimsuit and runs downstairs, obviously suspicious. I hear an "oh shit!" and fly down the stairs. Janis's mouth is wide open, her head dropped back, and her eyes closed.

"Make sure she's still breathing! I'm getting the Narcan!" Ocielle yells as she runs upstairs.

"Oh God! Do you want me to call—"

"No! Do whatever you want, but don't do that!" I'd forgotten about the illegalities being committed all around me and how calling 911 would inevitably lead to a search and seizure and probable arrests for everyone except Orlando and me—if he doesn't have any warrants, but I just met him two days ago. When you're intertwined in the narco world, your priorities shift from saving someone you care about to saving your own ass and staying out of prison.

I keep talking to Janis, slapping her face gently to make sure she's alive. Her lips are turning a faint blue, and random moans come out of her mouth.

"Oh, shit. Come on, Janis. Stay with me!" More uncomfortable moans come. I look at the syringe on the floor. She's overdosed and is dying right in front of me.

"Come on, Janis. You're okay." I try not get emotional as I watch her head move slowly to the left and right. I attempt to give her mouth to mouth, the only kind I know from watching people do it on television.

"Ocielle, hurry!" I scream. Janis's eyelids drop farther and farther down, and her breathing has slowed to a minimum. "Oh my God!"

"Okay, move. I got it," says Ocielle, pushing me out of the way. She is holding Narcan, the nasal spray that paramedics (and Ocielle) give to people who've overdosed on pain medications or heroin. She pumps four times into each nostril.

"Come on, girl. Wake up for me," she says. Janis moans again; her heart rate starts to pick up. I'm watching from the side. Gratefully, her eyes start to flutter open.

"Yes! That's it!"

"Come on, Janis!" we yell, cheering her on. She pulls her head up on her own, opens her eyes, and looks around. Ocielle and I hug her, elated. We've just saved someone's life, but Janis frowns.

"What the fuck?"

"You overdosed! We rescued you! You need to be more careful. This is the second time this week!" Ocielle says. "You need someone to monitor your intake or…"

Janis jumps to her feet, pushing her chair so hard it falls backward. "What the fuck, O? You totally ruined my high!"

"What the fuck? Are you serious? Seriously, get the fuck over it." An angry Ocielle marches back upstairs.

"Why'd you let her do that?" Janis asks me.

"Well, A, I didn't know what she was doing, and B, the way our brains operate is if someone in front of you is dying, you fucking *save* them."

"How dramatic. I wasn't going to die. I'm fine. Trust me. If I haven't overdosed by now, then I probably can't. My tolerance is through the roof at this point. I mean, look at my goddamn leg, and I'm *still* using. Probably the longest user here." She says it as if she deserved a medal.

"Well, your head was back, and your tongue was moving around, and you were moaning like you were in pain. It looked like you had a stroke. It's a pretty scary thing to witness."

"That was the best high ever though. Now it's gone, wasted."

"Yeah, because you were *dying*."

"I wasn't dying."

"You would have."

"Doubt it. Now I need more. Fuck," Janis says, opening her fanny pack.

"Are you fucking kidding me?"

One thing I've learned in my experience with addicts is there is no getting through to an active user.

"That Narcan's gonna cost you, Janis! That shit ain't cheap!" says Ocielle.

"How much?"

"A quarter ounce."

"Fuck off. Are you serious? I don't have that much, O."

"Then give me what you got. You've been doing too much anyway lately."

I look at Janis. She rolls her eyes.

"Fuck off," says Janis.

"Excuse me? I know you didn't just say that to me, you stupid little cunt!" Ocielle says.

Janis sticks her two middle fingers in the air and stomps outside. I wait fearfully, unsure whether Ocielle's going to come downstairs with a loaded AK-47 on a hunt for Janis.

I sneak out the front door. Orlando smokes on the porch, watching everyone pick up the orange caps, broken spoons, Coke bottles, candy wrappers, and dead lighters. They have sticks and black plastic bags like prisoners on the grassy knolls of highways.

It takes everyone a good thirty seconds to pick up a single Coke bottle or syringe cap, making the relatively easy task look excruciating and tedious. Addicts are good at being angry, especially at everyone but themselves. Currently they're angry because they have to pick up their own mess, and are arguing about who's the bigger slob. There's a "your mama" joke made by Prince. They struggle with their fanny packs getting in the way of the trash retrieval process, and profanities are shouted as it happened. Jimi takes his kit off and puts it around his neck so it isn't in the way.

"Look at 'em go," says Orlando. "They'll be here all night at that pace."

"Probably," I say.

"Yeah, well, it's not like they're not going anywhere. Fucking slobs. I mean, look at all that shit," says Ocielle, walking over to Orlando. I turn, surprised to see her. Luckily, she is weapon-free. She grabs Orlando's cigarette from his mouth, takes a drag, and hands it back to him as the three of us sit and watch Prince, Janis, Amy, Marilyn, Kurt, and Jimi all slowly maneuver their ways around the property.

"Well, at least I don't have to count my steps and touch shit before I can do anything," says Kurt, jokingly to Prince.

"Well, at least I'm not stupid enough to put a needle in my arm, trashy-ass mothafucka." We all giggle.

"Oh, right, you just put it up your nose," snarks Jimi.

"Oh, you're just so much better than us, Prince," says Janis. "Besides, aren't you kind of old to still be an addict? I feel like older folks should have their shit together by the time they're your age," she says, smiling and putting an empty box of foil in her trash bag.

"Girl says to me. You're the one who looks like her leg got mauled by a goddamn polar bear."

"Would y'all shut up and clean?" yells Ocielle from the porch.

"Where's Carlos?" asks Orlando. I'm surprised he's suddenly interested in Ocielle after she takes another drag of his cigarette and this time puts it back in his mouth.

"To work. Drop off another shipment," Ocielle says.

"So he's a trafficker?"

"Yeah, works for my dad. He used to be around a lot more, but when the states started legalizing marijuana…"

"What do you mean?"

"More competition to move heroin since marijuana isn't as in demand. More competition means more murders in my country. I'm not sure what would happen in Mexico if heroin gets legalized in the United States. That would…be the death of our economy."

"Ew, why is there a condom out here?" shrieks Marilyn.

"So Carlos has to really put the overtime hours in now, huh?" asks Orlando.

"Yep. Since the marijuana farmers have taken a hit, they started growing opium plants instead—dealing with new enemies, trying to take over our territories. But you know, it's sad, because the more doctors prescribe opiates, the longer my family will be in business, so it benefits us if they keep fucking up and overprescribing. The cartels should, like, partner with the pharmaceutical companies, you know? Like, keep pushing the pills! We should pay them. If it wasn't for them, well, we'd probably go broke."

"Damn, that's true. Sad but true. They're scared shitless of withdrawals," I say.

"I know, right? Like, how bad could it be?" Ocielle asks us, sitting down on the steps. She's changed into a tight lime-green miniskirt and black Bebe top. Hair and makeup fresh. Eyebrows and lips full, cheeks and chin contoured. I try to figure out what personality Ocielle is this afternoon. Either Yesenia or Shirley, thankfully. I don't know how much longer I can deal with a grown woman acting like a toddler.

"Pretty bad," says Orlando.

"You feel like you have the flu and want to crawl out of your skin. Not to mention the nausea and diarrhea. But I withdrew from Xanax by myself in my best friend's bed in college. So yeah, it sucks. Gave me seizures." The realization hits me. "Oh my God."

"What?" ask Orlando and Ocielle.

"It has to be epilepsy, what I have."

"You can still get seizures from alcohol and Xanax withdrawals alone," says Orlando.

"I know, but I've still had them for no reason, even before I swallowed anything. They've just changed form…if that's possible."

"You have epilepsy?" asks Ocielle.

"Maybe. Actually left Dallas to come to El Paso to find out what's wrong with me, and it looks like I've received my first probable diagnosis here on Contin Farm! Screw the doctors. We need real people with real experiences."

"They give Xanax to epileptics though, right?"

"Maybe. How ironic would that be? Someone who gets addicted to a benzo but actually needs it to live but gets addicted to it…I don't know. I first told my mom I needed Xanax when I was eight."

Orlando laughs and looks at me.

"Really though, if Xanax is used for epilepsy and I have epilepsy…I mean, what do you do in that situation, if you get addicted to the drug you need to not have seizures?"

"God, look at her leg," Orlando says, ignoring my epiphany. "How does that even happen?" Ocielle explains what she knows about krokodil, a cannibalistic form of heroin with all sorts of chemicals. The gaping wound on Janis's leg is deep and raw but not bleeding. Just her skin has rotted, revealing layers of pink and red flesh to the bone. Ocielle says some people get mold-like, circular patches on their skin, or it eats itself to the core, then turns black. The closest thing to a real-life horror movie you can find.

Ocielle stands, looking around at the expansive desert skin and sky in front and behind the house. The pink-and-purple setting sky is magnificent, as are the clouds cradling the setting globe in orange and yellow shades.

"Okay, y'all are good," she yells, cupping her mouth to project her voice.

Chapter 31

Just a Rat in a Cage

I hope I can dial out way out here in the West. I borrow Orlando's phone to call my parents to hear the status of the intervention. Cell service is almost nonexistent, and since I'm calling Dallas, I'm sure…wait…it's ringing!

"Hello, this is Hugo."

"Hey, Dad. What are you doing?"

"Oh my God. Delores, it's Poppy! What the hell? Are you okay? Where are you?" he asks. "You coming home yet?"

"Yeah, Dad, relax. I accidentally dropped my phone in the toilet, so it sort of…doesn't work."

"What the hell are you doing, Poppy? Your dad and I have been worried sick." My mom has obviously snatched the phone away.

"Relax, y'all. I'm fine. Seriously, I hardly have connection out here, and my phone probably wouldn't get service where I am anyway."

I tell them most of the truth about how I met Orlando and that we went to high school together, so they'll be less likely to assume the worst when I use the dooming term "hitchhiker." I'm sure all parents would love to hear about how their daughter picked up some cute guy on the side of the road. I am questioning how my dad will perceive the situation, knowingly wanting to help addicts in need but not wanting to refuse someone else the possibility of getting help because *he* admitted a bunch of people his daughter found in West Texas with million-dollar interiors but Section 8 exteriors.

"How bad are they? Do they *want* to get clean?"

"Some, I think. It's hard to tell. I really think some don't know anything about the program, so if we could get Ryan or Charlie to intervene or just give them a rundown of what addiction is and Suboxone and all that. I would, but it might make the situation worse if I slam them with an intervention and nowhere to take them."

He sighs loudly on the other end. When treatment at his facility is $500 a day, he has a right to be anxious, debating the loss of income but doing me and especially those who want to go to treatment a life-altering favor.

"How many again?"

"Only a few, I'd imagine. Six at the most, if no one dies before you get here."

"Wow. That bad, huh?"

"Yeah, like an apocalypse. Everyone you talk to is either high or shooting up, wandering around like zombies. The girl who owns the house is the daughter of a drug kingpin in Juarez. She sleeps with a guy who brings her an insane amount of dope, and the residents do things for her so she pays them in dope! It's crazy, like a summer camp for junkies."

My dad is speechless, which never happens. He whispers "wow" about four times. He tells me he'll call the interventionists and see what their thoughts were, and if they agree, they'll leave tomorrow morning. Orlando and I need to stay again tonight.

Orlando and I sit on the porch, watching the sunset as everyone goes back inside. I get a closer look at Janis's leg as she passes us. I can't help but be fascinated by the repulsive krokodil epidemic.

"What'd your dad say?" he asks, looking around to make sure everyone is inside.

"Um, that he'd be willing to do it, just needs to have a conversation with the interventionists about coming out tomorrow. There *should* be enough beds if everyone wants to go, but I'm sure they won't."

"Who do you think will?"

"That's a rough call. You never know. But if I had to guess…"

I tell him I think Prince will go, since he mentioned something to me earlier about really wanting his family back. Jimi I doubt, because he says he's in love with Ocielle and feels doomed to the life of an addict. I guess Kurt will go so he can hopefully go pro, and Janis might go but wouldn't stay sober. Since Marilyn feeds off the approval of Ocielle, her recovery might all depend on how Ocielle feels about them going to treatment. She is a good soul but a codependent in its purest form. She wants friends, and this is the only way she knows how to have them. They are her lifeline. In recovery it's said that codependents are just as sick as the addicts, and Ocielle is the sickest of them all.

Ocielle opens the door and peeks her head out, asking whether we've seen Jimi. When we tell her no, Orlando stands up to get water and to pee and passes Janis on his way in. I notice the sunlight changing; it's that time of day again. The needles on the ground. I might throw up. I smell something sulfury. It's back. I'm powerless.

"Orlando!" I scream, horrified. He runs back outside.

"It's back. Hand me my purse," I say, taking deep breaths. Janis walks outside, which makes it worse. My brain is on overdrive and can't handle it.

"Do you have any…opioids?" I ask Janis. My arm is curling; my insides feel as if they were on fire; the colors of the sky change from pitch black to orange and pink to black again.

"No! NO, ma'am! She doesn't mean that," says Orlando to a speechless Janis. The porch feels as if it were sliding underneath me. I hold on to the wooden steps. Orlando hands me a pill and some water. I can feel my eyelid twitching.

"How pretty is the sky, though?" I ask, feeling tingly and glowing, as if there were a light surrounding me.

"It's very nice. Can I go inside now?" Orlando asks.

"Um, duh, yeah! I never said you couldn't. Thank you, Orlan-DOE!" I'm unsure whether I feel better because I just took a Valium or because the episode is actually over. Either way, it doesn't matter; I'm back again where I left off.

"Hey. What's your name again?" Janis asks, digging in her purple fanny pack. Her tattered Converse have all sorts of graffiti and holes, and she has thin line scars on her bony ankle. She sits down in Orlando's spot next to me.

"Hey! I'm Poppy. You?"

"Hey. Um, my name's Janis," she says, distracted by her tools. She dumps the heroin on a spoon and puts fire to the bottom. Her eyes light up in excitement. She takes her syringe and sucks up the thin, white juice. "How'd you know Ocielle?" she asks.

"I don't. I mean, I didn't. I just heard...about it, this place."

"Where there's a bunch of junkies, living basically for free in a mansion?" She wraps some blue painting tape around her bicep as she searches her arm madly. "Shit veins, where are you, where are you? Eh, fuck, these are dead. Maybe this one..."

"Something like that. We're just seeing the sights, you know. Passing through."

"You use dope or just Valium?" she asks, eyeing my veins and arms for wear and tear. She inserts the needle into the side of her neck. "Yes, yes, that's it!"

"No, I don't use dope. I was given the Valium for my attacks, like you witnessed. Obviously, they don't prevent them, but I guess when I take them..."

"Yeah, I got you," she says, grabbing the back of her knees as she slowly rocks back and then up with her eyes closed and mouth wide open. The stars start poking through the dark blanket of the desert sky to say hello.

"Does it hurt? Your leg?"

"Yeah, like a fucking bitch. That desomorphine shit is no joke. Got it from a friend once, did it a few times...like...then it literally...like...eats...you for lunch. Chomp." She begins to hum, and she buries her head into her knees.

"Have you ever wanted to get sober?" I ask.

"I mean, yeah, been to detox like ten times...but...always...chase...the dragon once I'm...out. It's so fucked. I'm such a piece of shit...I was literally shooting up on the...bathroom floor...at my first couple treatment centers, and the ones I wouldn't, I'd do it right when I got out."

"So you weren't ready then. No big deal. Most people aren't when they go to treatment."

"That's what they say, ye know. Keep comin' back. It works…"

"If *you* work *it*. The program's not gonna ring your doorbell and be like, 'Hello, the twelve steps are here, ready for *you* to go on a journey with us. Please be our guest. If the road gets a little uncomfortable, please let us know, and we'll stop.'"

Janis manages a laugh and compliments me on my English accent.

"Yeah. I mean, I would go to meetings and want to *want* to not get high but…I dunno, I guess my bottom is six feet under. It's my destiny, you know? My…pops…was…an addict, my uncle. It's in my blood. They've…paved the way for me. Plus…what would my life be if I got sober? Boring. I wouldn't feel like this."

"I mean, so what, are you busy filling your days with meaningful and interesting activities that feed your soul? It looks like you're doing the same thing over and over again every single day. To me, *that's* boring."

"This is my…my identity. Like, I've been an addict for so long now, and I have this leg…it's…just…who I am."

"Sure, I hear you. You can change, though, break the mold. It's hard. The debate of living a normal life and being a productive citizen versus a junkie life doing the same thing every day, hoping one day you'll wake up and it or you will be different, is the war in every addict's mind. You just need to get to a desperation when you realize, 'No matter how bored I think I'll get or be in sobriety, it has to be a life better than this.'"

An addict's whole world revolves around getting the next batch or getting the money for it somehow, not to get high but to not get sick. In a lot of cases, getting high is a thing of the past. Their bodies are reliant on the drug. When your body is reliant on something, relationships, goals, and responsibilities fall to the wayside when the end goal is not to be happy but to be high.

A part of the addict wants the calmness and normality and honest achievement that comes with being clean, but another part of the soul craves the chaos, the unpredictability, drama, and numbness.

"The junkie girl…that's me. Hey…if something…happens to me, don't…go get Ocielle, okay? Don't bring me back. Please. Ohh…this is good shit, girl." There is a long pause. I watch her enjoying herself.

"Okay, I won't," I say hesitantly. She flicks the ashes off her barely touched Newport.

"You know, addiction…is…the…only…qualm that enables you to break your *own* heart?" she asks, still rocking with her eyes closed.

"Yeah, and the only disease that tells you you don't have it," I add, gazing at the sky and stars. The wind is cool and clear. "But yeah, breaking your own heart. I get that. Never heard that before, but it is really such a self-betrayal. When you have no control over your own actions, I mean, that just…"

"Suuuucks," she says. "Like, I went into detox ten months ago, after I got arrested, and I was done. I thought I was. You know…it was, like, my third possession charge, and I was looking at some time…I was all, 'No, no more. This is it. I'm getting on Suboxone. I'm done,' and meant it…like, with…every fiber of my being."

"Yeah, what happened?"

"Well, funny story. When I bailed out, I was walking to the clinic, and I ran into one of my dealers from, like, three years ago. I was shocked he was still alive, you know? Heroin doesn't preserve the user for very long. Like, once you start shooting, like, right then your death clock starts…ticking."

"Did you tell your dealer you were quitting or…"

"Yeah! I did actually, now that I think about it. Sure fuckin' did, and he didn't take me seriously. Was all like, 'Well, you just got out of jail. Let's go get high. You can sober up tomorrow or the next day.' And that was, like, I dunno. A long time ago."

"And the next day never came, I'm assuming?"

"Hell no, it never does for heroin addicts, no. It's always, 'Oh, I'll quit before I start prostituting' or 'I'll quit next week because I got court' or whatever. Just flimsy excuses to feel better about themselves, but deep down they know. They know they're not going to quit. Something inside of you tells you, like, 'Shut up. You know you're not done.' It literally screams at you…for me, at least."

"Oh yeah, trust me, I know. The devil's voice—your inner critic. Or the addict's voice or whatever you call it. I think it's there for all addicts and alcoholics. We want to *want* to be done, and we know we should. It just…doesn't happen that way." Some days it seems as if you're winning and making strides, and then out of nowhere the rug is pulled out underneath your feet, and you can't explain why. I look at Janis, who is still holding her knees to her chest and rocking gently back and forth with her head back and eyes closed.

"Yeah. I've been waiting to want to want it, but…I dunno." After a few silent minutes together, she begins to sing.

"Despite all my rage…I am…still…just a…rat in a cage." I sit silently as her inhales become further and further apart. I start to worry.

There's a time in all young adult lives when we're asked to make decisions we're too inexperienced to respond to wisely. This is one of those moments. I have eight thousand feelings and emotions. Janis says she wants to lie down on the porch. Her inhales are now about thirty seconds apart. Her heart is stopping. I instinctively want to leap to my feet to call 911 or Ocielle to get the Narcan, but I told her I wouldn't.

Chapter 32

El Condor Pasa

"Have you seen Orlando?" I ask Ocielle, who is sprawled out on the couch watching *The Bachelor* with Marilyn, who has nodded out with her head back on the sofa. She looks at Marilyn.

"Hey! Wake up!" Ocielle nudges Marilyn's fanny pack with her bare foot. "I think he's upstairs in the arcade," she tells me.

"Okay, thanks." I get upstairs quickly, trying not to cause suspicion.

"Hey! Oh my God. I was talking to that Janis girl just now, and I think she might have died. She told me not to tell Ocielle to bring her back with the Narcan, so we should respect that. But wow, how fucked is that? Oh my God."

He stops playing and shuts the door. "Surely you told her to fuck off, right? Why didn't you tell Ocielle she was right there?" he asks in an aggressive whisper, slightly perspiring from the physical activity in the game room.

"I dunno. Because she told me not to. Look, the girl wanted to die, Orlando."

"Oh my God, they don't know what they want! They're addicts! Basically children. Where is she?"

"Oh my God!" We hear the screaming from downstairs. We look at each other and bolt down to the front yard. Jimi and Marilyn are hunched over her with their heads in their hands.

"Oh my God, really, Janis?" says Ocielle, cupping her mouth.

"She's gone. She's cold," says Jimi. Amy walks over to see what the screaming is about.

"Great Caesar's ghost! Tell me what I am looking at is not real this moment!" Amy shrieks. No one pays her any attention, too shocked by what's happened. She collapses to the ground in a fit. "Janis, no! Janis, no!" she yells in tears. Tears glide down my face as I look at her pale body, and I can't help but feel guilty and powerlessness over my decision to keep quiet. She didn't want to be saved, she didn't want to be saved, I keep saying to myself.

"I'll get the shovel," says Prince, walking back to the house.

"How could you do such a thing to me?" Amy asks the corpse with blurry eyes. Orlando looks at me and shakes his head.

"Fuck you," I mouth to him.

"She already has a cross made," says Ocielle.

"What the FUCK!" yells Amy. "Why would you make her a cross?" she asks.

"Um, because it's a nice thing to do, and I'm a nice person?" fires Ocielle, offended. Ocielle making crosses for everyone, in her mind, is the equivalent of a kindergarten teacher making name tags for her students. Orlando's mouth and mine are wide open in shock. Prince walks back with a shovel and a cross.

"Wait, you're really going to?" I ask.

"Yeah, Poppy," says Jimi. "Funerals are expensive. Plus Ocielle says this is the best way to do it because of the earth's natural decomposing elements." I roll my eyes.

"Would you mind? My back is killing me," Prince says as he hands the shovel to Orlando.

"You're kidding."

"Would you…really mind? You're the most athletic one here. Last time it took Jimi two hours to dig a four-foot grave," Prince whispers.

"I'll be right back, promise, y'all," says Prince as he heads in the direction of the house.

"Where the hell is he going?" I ask.

"To wash his hands twice and sanitize," say Marilyn, Ocielle, Jimi, Kurt, and Amy in unison.

Orlando stands in shock, holding the shovel. I can almost hear his thoughts exploding,

153

deciding whether he is going to be a participant in the burial or throw down the shovel, shout profanities, and start walking back to Tucson.

Ocielle tells Orlando to consider it while she goes inside to change clothes for the funeral. Currently she's casually dressed in jeans and a Dallas Cowboys T-shirt with a cracking star logo stretched to the max so it can fit over her enlarged chest.

Ocielle comes back with a CD player, Agnes, and Missy the tiger on a leash, wearing fairy wings and a tight black dress. Everyone is clearly used to Missy, or they're too high to care or notice. The spandex dress reflects the midafternoon sun, making her plasticized behind look like a soiled diaper on steroids. With all the bizarre shit buzzing around me, I'm surprised I don't have an attack. I have a deceased woman, a tiger, and a grown woman who is suddenly a five-year-old toddler.

"Holy shit!" says Orlando, looking at Missy.

"She doesn't bite. Only the bad people," says Ocielle in her baby voice. She sets down Agnes, the Cabbage Patch doll. "Come on, Orlando. I've let you stay in my house for two nights for free, with food *and* dessert." Her lips are pressed tightly together, with fire in her eyes. "Missy doesn't like it when people don't support the family. She gets real mad. You don't want to make Missy mad!"

"Whatever. Fine. Where? But I'm not fucking lowering her in," he says defiantly. Big cats held in captivity rarely attack, and obviously Ocielle doesn't know that Prince let Orlando feed Missy earlier, so he's not a stranger or a threat to her, or he shouldn't be.

"Plot number twelve?" I hadn't realized the graves were numbered. We all walk over silently, powerlessly, unsure what the future holds from this moment forward. Orlando gives me a sour look as if to say that this is my fault. Amy unzips her fanny pack, gets out her dope, a syringe, cotton, water, a spoon, and a lighter. Orlando begins digging a hole, and Amy and Kurt begin digging for a vein.

"Agnes, can you help that Orlando man dig the hole?" Ocielle asks her doll. "No? Okay, me neither. He will make a nice, great big hole so it will keep Janis nice and warm forever." I want to vomit when I see her eyes light up as she talks to her doll. I hear a noise behind me and see Jimi and Prince carrying Janis's body in a white sheet. Prince now wears a three-piece purple suit and matching hat, while Jimi is in ripped jeans, flip-flops, and a flannel shirt. I, on the other hand, didn't pack for a funeral, so I'm stranded in white linen pants and a bleached denim shirt. Poor Orlando's been in his faded jeans and white shirt for two whole days now.

He digs a decent-size plot in about ten minutes.

"I can't believe I'm doing this," he says, wiping the sweat off his forehead and lighting a cigarette. "Hey, Kurt or Jimi, can someone get me some water please? At least do something besides gossiping about sports and Eva Longoria while there's a corpse literally a foot behind you."

"Fuck you, bro. You don't know us," says Kurt. Orlando stops.

"Ha. I don't know you? Trust me: I know you. You're a bunch of pussies who can't stop whining or feeling sorry for yourself long enough to sober up." They look at him, perplexed. "You're all just like my brother," he says, putting his hair in a man bun while everyone waits to see what he'll say next. I'm more worried about the intervention set for tomorrow. If he keeps this shit up, we'll get escorted off the property, and there will be no intervention.

"'Poor me, I have to use heroin every hour because I was abused, and now I can't get sick, so I just have to keep using.' Or 'Ouchie, poor me, my tooth really hurts. Now I need eight hundred Percocets until it feels better!' But my favorite one is 'I lost my kids, so I guess I'll keep using heroin try to get them back, since that's exactly what I did to lose them.'"

Everyone falls silent. I can't believe he sank that low. I'm not sure whether he knows that's Amy's story. I'm afraid to look at her, and mouth to Orlando to stop.

I slowly turn my head, grateful to see Amy has nodded off, as if she fell asleep trying to smell the clouds. For all anyone knows, she could even be dead. Prince's mouth is open in excitement, but nothing comes out.

"That's…fucked up, bro," says Kurt, pulling his head up.

Then Jimi follows Kurt, saying, "Yeah. Fuck yeah, it is."

"Okay, kids, that's enough!" says Prince, turning on the CD player to shift the mood as Ocielle sprints inside, saying she's going to get water for Orlando.

When Simon and Garfunkel start playing and Prince starts tapping his foot, anxiety quickly builds in my stomach, as if someone just ran up behind me, pushing me off a cliff. Maybe what triggered it is a mix of Orlando losing it and the thought of me being alone in the middle of West Texas with a bunch of junkies and a cartel spawn with no phone. Or that there is a car en route to slam them with an intervention. My brain can't handle all the emotion and excitement.

"Damnit," I say loudly as my brain starts flipping before everything goes patchy and black and it starts turning inside out. The anxiety gets stronger, as well as the sudden depression. I need to shake my feet because they're asleep, but I am too terrified to move, afraid any sudden movement can injure my delicate brain and make it stick in spell mode. Similar to the fear you get when your mom tells you as a kid your face will get stuck that way. I am sure every time my brain will get stuck this way.

"Ugh, I hate these so much. Hang on, gimme a sec. Okay, this one might kill me. I feel like I'm going to die."

"What? No, Poppy, you're fine," says Orlando, the only one concerned. With all the bizarre antics these people see on the daily, my spells are child's play to them.

"Get me my Valium," I demand.

"See, I bet you that's the seizure," says Jimi, whose head is raised. Orlando stops digging and gets the Valium from my bag.

"Do you have water?" I ask someone, I'm not sure who. "Can you get me water, please? I can't breathe. Or alcohol. A drink." My hand wants to curl for some reason, and I crouch down, unable to stand, since I can't see reality anymore. Ocielle runs back outside with two bottles of water for Orlando and me when his phone goes off. I am staring off into space, certain it will never stop. Moments later the beautiful euphoria starts to creep in, and everything is back to its normal coloring, which is brighter than I remember from before, and everyone is beautiful and healthy.

I look at what I am holding.

"Why do I have a bottle of water?" I ask.

"You said you hated these things and that you couldn't breathe and asked me to get your Valium. Ocielle came back with water."

"Oh no, I asked you for water?" I laugh. "Sorry, Ocielle, but thank you. You're the best."

"I thought you said you didn't drink," she says.

"I don't. Why?"

"Because you asked me for alcohol."

"Oh shit, did I really? You didn't give me any though, right?"

"No, because you told me earlier you quit a few years ago because you had a spiritual malady. So which is it?"

"No, I don't drink. I just…when I have these spells or whatever they are, I say things I don't mean to say. It's weird. I can't help it. It's only ever about drugs and alcohol though, I think….at least that's what others have said."

"Yeah, Jimi says you might be epileptic," says Orlando, sitting on the ground next to me.

"That sounds just awful, doesn't it?" I ask, envisioning what it would be like to actually have epilepsy, starting to feel the fatigue from the Valium.

I tell Prince he can turn the music back on. We are ready to begin. After "Bridge over Troubled Water" comes on, Ocielle yells to Prince that the song is track number eight.

Vincent van Gogh was reportedly an epileptic who cut off his ear during a seizure and ran down the streets naked. Would I need to get a wheelchair? Would my driver's license be revoked? I did get in an accident on my way here. The madness has to end.

I ask Orlando to borrow his phone and tell them to wait for me. I need to get the status of the intervention before everyone living here overdoses.

"Hello?"

"Hey, it's me. Where are y'all?" I whisper, grateful that service comes easy.

"Hey, Pop, your mom and I and Ryan are on our way. We're about a couple hours out."

"Okay, just hurry. Earlier a girl OD'd right in front of me, and they have this graveyard for everyone who's overdosed and died here. Crosses and everything."

"Wow. I just can't believe we haven't heard about this place on the news or something. But we are on our way. Just occupy yourselves for a little longer." I can hear my mom saying something in the background. "Oh, and stay with your friend with the phone, your mother says. Tell your friend I'll pay him for helping you. Is there a physical address to where you are?"

"Not that I can see. She wants it as low key as possible, so I doubt it. There's nothing around the house. I think the nearest gas station is a QuikTrip that's, like, a mile from here. But it's the only large house on the side of the highway that looks abandoned, but it's not. You should see the inside. Oh, by the way, I was talking to this guy here, and he said that he thinks I'm epileptic, that I'm actually having seizures and not panic attacks, like the doctors thought."

"We'll look into that more when we get back to Dallas."

"Yeah. Like how I curl my hand up and smack my lips and flutter my eyelashes? Apparently that's a seizure."

"Yeah, maybe. But right now I'm more concerned with you being with some strange boy you said you went to high school with."

"He's not a weirdo, I promise. Or a serial killer, as far as I can see, but the night is young!" I say, smiling.

"Poppy, that's not funny!"

"But I gotta go. I'm sure Orlando wants me off his phone. Text this number, and keep me updated, okay?"

"Yep. See you. Stay safe!"

I walk back to the gravesite, where everyone is alive again (except Janis) and chatting, including Orlando. Hopefully they'll forgive him for his harsh monologue and not tell Amy about his offensive statement so it won't sabotage the intervention.

"Well, it doesn't matter. My identical twin brother died from alcohol poisoning two years ago, almost to the day, so sorry if I'm a little sensitive on the subject of addicts and addiction. I just don't buy into it," he says.

"Well, you're lucky you didn't get the gene," I say.

"Seriously? You're a twin?" asks Marilyn.

"Yep. Was. But he couldn't give up the booze. Then this piece of shit let him try heroin. Wasn't the same since."

"How old was he?" asks Jimi.

"Umm, he died when he was twenty-seven."

"I can't imagine," says Marilyn.

"Yeah, thanks, most people can't. It's cool, but it's still hard. Sorry I snapped, by the way. But it just brings back bad memories…this whole place, this…disease." He casually pretends to rub his eyes, but I'm sure he's shedding tears. Men do that. Kurt, Jimi, and Amy stand up to carry Janis's body to the hole. Prince is still playing with the radio.

"I told you 'El Condor Pasa' is numero eight!" shouts Ocielle, braiding Agnes's hair and occasionally speaking to her.

"Whoa, nelly. You need to relax, young lady."

"Pasta? What? You're playing a song about *pasta*?" asks Marilyn, confused. I try not to laugh, but I can't help it.

"PA-ZZAAA! You idiot. Haven't you ever heard of Simon and Garfunkel?" Says Ocielle.

"No, but I'm not, like, thirty, like your old ass."

Bagpipes start sounding; Prince found it. Ocielle's face lights up.

"Everyone, grab hands!" yells Ocielle. She instructs us to circle around Janis's grave as Kurt covers her with the sheet and then dirt. Everyone grabs hands and circles the grave. After the prayer Ocielle says to walk in a circle three times around the grave, like some nineteenth-century voodoo shit. Ocielle even finishes with a little kick, nearly knocking over her fairy wings.

Ocielle grabs the cross and forces it into the dirt like an ice pick into a block of ice.

"Hot tub, anyone?" she asks.

Chapter 33

Saunas and Scams

"That was weird, huh?" Orlando asks me, putting on Carlos's swim trunks.

"Yeah, pretty fucked. This should be the last day we're here until my folks arrive."

"Thank God. I don't know how much more insanity I can take."

Luckily, Ocielle likes her bikini tops super tiny, and mine probably barely covers her nipples but covers the whole shebang when I put it on. The bikini bottom's strings are tied to the max on the sides, with the strings hanging to my knees.

"Nice," says Orlando, looking at me.

"Shut up."

His creamy, hairy white thighs are in full view in Carlos's neon trunks.

"You go outside at all or…" I say, smiling.

"Fuck you. These are a little shorter than I'd normally wear. Sue me. Plus I'm doing this crap for you."

"And my dad's paying you."

"And your dad *is* paying me. Let's get this awkward stupid experience over with."

The smell of chlorine and bleach waft through the air after Ocielle punches the code to get in. It's just us three; the others are still changing, I assume.

In the lap pool floats a figure with brown hair facedown, causing me to jump back.

"Relax. It's a doll," says Ocielle, giggling.

"Oh my God. That looks just like a person. Like…that's not a Barbie butt. That's someone's real ass! Why do you have a life-size doll in the pool?" I create an echo.

"Carlos was into it a few months ago. Me, him, and dolly. She wasn't cheap either. Whatever I got to do to make my customers happy, you know?" she says, turning on the hot tub. I look at Orlando, who's immune to the madness at this point.

"Hello?" We turn and look to see Amy, Jimi, and Kurt have arrived, holding towels.

"Hey, I'm just turning it on. It's still a little cool but warm enough to get in."

Prince comes in, still wearing his fanny pack and a black Speedo.

"Good afternoon to ya!"

"Hey, Prince. We're just warming the tub up," says Ocielle. I try not to look at the others in their swimwear but can't unsee what I see. Bruises in the pits of their elbows, red spots, and scars are all over the bodies of Amy, Marilyn, Jimi, and Kurt. One of the reasons junkies are usually wearing long sleeves and pants is because of the bruising and scarring that comes with the nature of the beast.

"Oh, it's good now," says Marilyn. Her body is so frail and bony in her one-piece. If a gust of wind comes, we may never see her again. Her eating disorder has made her bones protrude; they appear massive, like a healthy grown male's. We step into the hot tub, which seats ten at least. The steam rises.

"Forgive me, but how old is that bruise?" I ask Marilyn, pointing to the pit of her elbow.

"Oh, um, that? I dunno, couple weeks maybe. Missed a vein. Again." Her voice is low and crawling, and her eyes are half-open. Kurt, Jimi, and Amy are enjoying themselves so much they're nodding out.

"Isn't this what heroin's like, anyway?" I ask them, getting their attention.

"Huh?" asks Kurt.

"Stepping into a hot tub. Isn't that what heroin feels like? That's what I've heard. Or getting hugged by an angel, or the thrill of going downhill on the tallest roller coaster in the world." Unsurprisingly, they all wake back up. Heroin is clearly the thing they seem to like to talk about.

"Yeah, that's a pretty good analogy," says Marilyn with her mouth open.

"Yeah, like the best orgasm ever," chimes Ocielle.

"How come you never do it, Ocielle?" I ask, suddenly feeling brave.

"Heroin? Fuck that shit. I basically grew up with it. Never did it, never cared. It was the thing in my mind that took my daddy away when I was five for three years, and not even because he did it. Maybe I should try it, see what it's like. See what all the hoopla is about." Amy is appalled by the statement.

"Well, with all my might, I beg of you to not. Once you start, you're a slave. You'll always want that high. You then destroy everything meaningful and honest in your life. There's no beauty without truth, and heroin is the ugliest dame in the castle! That's what life as an addict is. A constant chase. You get high. Then you wonder when you're going to get high again, and where you'll get the money, and where the dealer is, and so on and on and on and on and on: get high, come down, find money, call the dealer. Get high, come down, find money, call the dealer. Get high, come down, find money, call the dealer. Get high, come down, find money, call the dealer. Get high, come down, find money, call the dealer. Get high, come down, find money, call the dealer, Get high, come down, find money, call the dealer—"

"That's enough!" shrieks Marilyn. Amy ignores her.

"It never stops, never ends, until you're six feet under. It's like being on a roller coaster you can't get off. It's awful...bloody miserable. It's a riot because I actually feel better about myself *before* I shoot up than after. We keep ourselves in our own desperate prisons, like hopeless insects in a spider web, powerless but refusing to admit total defeat." We're all shocked by Amy's candor. It's more than I've heard her say in almost three whole days put together.

"Well, you *do* know heroin addicts can get sober though, right, Amy?" I say. "You can get off the roller coaster when you have the realization that you will *always be on it*, it will never get better, it will only get astounding worse. That is, unless you decide you're worth pulling yourself up off the ocean floor and trying something new."

"I don't think I'm an addict though. I just don't want to quit. Like, I'm choosing not to quit. Why would I? I have my friends, I work, I got immediate access, I got a spicy Latina," says Kurt. Ocielle blushes. Orlando makes a noise as if he can't take it anymore and slips underwater.

"Well, for me at least," I say, "I think it was not being okay with looking into the mirror and being confused about who I'd become, almost overnight. I remember that night so clearly. I was having a going-away party—for myself, of course, alcoholics are narcissists to the core—at a restaurant in North Beach in San Francisco. When I excused myself to go to the bathroom, I washed my hands and looked into my eyes in the mirror. I could see in my eyes that my soul had turned black. I was sleeping with a lot of men I didn't know, not even for money but for fun. I was drinking and I didn't want to, but figured I obviously *wanted* to. Otherwise I wouldn't drink or do drugs! I learned several years later that I was drinking against my own will. Especially when I really tried to have two or three and I had fifteen. I kept thinking I was the one in control and changing my mind, but my mind was changed for me by alcohol. I was powerless every time I drank over how many I'd consume. I am powerless over living life by my own free will alone and being happy…or surviving."

"Fuccck, dude," says Jimi, "how old were you?"

"I hit a bottom a few times, but…twenty. I stayed sober when I was twenty-two."

"Alcohol though, you can't be good with two?" asks Ocielle. "What about, have you tried, like, drinking water between drinks?" I've been asked this question maybe fifty times in my life.

"Water would dilute the alcohol. Plus it's not a contest over whoever is the drunkest is the alcoholic, but who can drink ten and stay stopped for days or weeks. Normal drinkers and heavy drinkers can; alcoholics cannot. It's not that I can't live with it in my life. It's that I can't live without it in my life that makes all the difference."

"I had an experience with that once," says Jimi. "I filled…one of those…Sonic Route

44 cups with, like, half Coke and half Jose Cuervo 'cause it was sitting out. I was, like…sixteen, and my mom found out, so she poured out, like, five thousand bucks' worth of my dad's pretentious aged wine and whiskeys and shit all down the drain. My dad was pissed." Everyone manages a laugh.

"And did the absence of alcohol stop you from drinking ever again?" I ask.

"Hell no. Well, I eventually got hurt, then got pills, then moved and couldn't get pills, so I started junk and don't really give a fuck about booze anymore."

"Well, you didn't stop drinking for good or using for good because the alcohol or heroin was gone, right?"

"Fuck no," Kurt and Jimi say. Marilyn and Amy nod their heads in agreeance.

"Right, because alcohol and heroin itself is not the problem. *We* are the problem. It's not that the alcohol is on the shelf or the heroin is in your pocket. It's that we, as addicts and alcoholics, can't do what we need to do and *not* use or drink. Otherwise, if it were alcohol's fault and shame be to it, then we'd still have Prohibition, but we don't, because ninety percent of the population can be around alcohol, buy it, drink an enormous quantity, and go to work the next day and function and be nice and work hard and not drink for a month."

Everyone is silent. Prince contributes.

"It seems, though, like when I try and control, like this is my last baggie of dope I'ma buy and then I'm gonna wait for two days before I get the dealer on the phone, but it never works that way, control. I just…can't."

"Yeah, that's the thing too. If addicts and alcoholics are trying to control their using or drinking, then they are not enjoying it. If they are enjoying it, they're not controlling it. Maybe you're an addict and maybe not, but just ask yourself that question. Can you control *and* enjoy at the same time?"

"So you, like, worked the steps or whatever, yeah?" asks Marilyn.

"Yes."

"Well, I get that, but the steps never worked for me. I dunno. Maybe I wasn't doing it right. But they don't work for me, I tell ya."

"Well, they've worked for millions of people who felt like that too. They'll work for you when you're finally done with being a slave and realize you're powerless to stay stopped. Until then, no, they won't work, but you have to know deep down you can't stop on your own, ever. Ever. Ever, ever, ever, ever. You *will never stop on your own if you're a true addict*. You won't wake up one day and be over it and just quit, so stop praying for that day, because it will never come."

Prince's face drops when I say this, and Kurt and Jimi are staring at me, trying to piece together what the hell I'm talking about in their altered state. Orlando excuses himself, telling me he has to pee, and kisses my forehead on his way in.

"Only a power greater than yourself can help you."

"I dunno. I mean, it just pulls me right back. Like, I'll be like, 'No, I'm really for real done,' and then my deelah would call me and tell about the new good shit he got, and I can't say no," says Kurt, his Boston accent shining through.

"I had a friend tell me once that it's the indecisiveness that will kill you. It's ultimately what eats us alive. We're meant to be whole, not divided individuals, spiritually and mentally. Not making up your mind, going back and forth, 'No, I wanna stop,' 'No, I stopped stopping.' That's the internal struggle that gnaws at your soul: indecisiveness. Go or stay. Fight or flight. Use or sober up. Win or lose. Kill or be killed."

Everyone is nodding except for Ocielle, who looks panicked. I need to halt the conversation before she gets suspicious.

"Are y'all hungry? I can make some food or something," I say, looking at Ocielle.

There is a possibility they will all refuse treatment in lieu of the mad pursuit of escaping reality, but I feel as if I got through to them. Even if they disagree, I just planted the seed. However, there is also a possibility that they all choose to divorce themselves from junk's potency and self-pity and choose to have a worthy existence from here on out. Although a trip to rehab isn't keeping anybody sober or making any promises, it's a positive beginning.

"Marilyn, when are you going to EP to get that money?" Asks Ocielle.

"What? Oh, really, again? I don't know. I guess after this hot tub party."

Marilyn has a special work suit she wears to pull this scam off. She looks like a professional in black pants and a black blazer with her makeup done perfectly. No one would ever know she was a junkie trying to get high. Right now, she's a professional missing her iPad. She walks into the lobby of a massive commercial real estate building, searching desperately for a security officer.

"Hi, has anyone turned in a black iPad Mini?" she asks the balding security man frantically.

"Nope, not to my knowledge."

"Oh my God, I have to find it! I'm going to get fired if it doesn't show up, and I have two kids at home to feed!"

"Okay, just calm down, ma'am. What kind was it? A black iPad?"

"Umm, it was a black Apple, yeah, with a case about an inch thick. I'll give whoever returns it, say, how much do I have, five hundred in cash. No questions asked."

"Five hundred in cash. All right, lemme write that down." The guard pulls out a mini spiral notepad and pen from his front shirt pocket.

"Here, let me leave you my number so you can call me when—if it even shows up. Oh God, I'm going to get fired," she says, writing down her number. He informs Marilyn he'll be on the lookout and call her right away if he has any information at all. She thanks him profusely and exits the foyer, smiling.

Two blocks down she spots Ocielle's car and Jimi and Kurt in the front.

"That was too easy. Who's going?" Marilyn asks.

"Jimi, it's your turn," says Kurt with heavy red eyes. "I did it last time."

"Dammit, okay. Gimme the thing." Kurt pulls out a broken iPad with a thick case from the glove box.

"It's the white balding security guard. I think he's the only one there."

"And the description?"

"A black iPad, I need it for work, five hundred in cash. I'll, umm, wait here," says Marilyn. Jimi takes his beanie off and runs his fingers through his hair and squirts in his eyes eye drops he has in his fanny pack.

"Don't, umm, don't forget that," says Marilyn, pointing to his fanny pack.

Inside, Jimi finds the guard immediately.

"Hey, I'm not sure if you're the person I give this to, but I found this outside on y'all's bench. Has anyone reported it? It's pretty nice just to leave. I'd assume someone would want it back."

"Oh yeah, that's great, thank you. A young woman came by about thirty minutes ago and said she really needed it for work and she's giving a five-hundred-dollar cash reward."

"Oh, no shit? Awesome! I can use five hundred—"

"Yeah, me too. That's why I told her I'd call her," the guard says, taking the device from Jimi.

"Wait, bro, I'm the one who found this. Shouldn't *I* get the reward?"

"Well, uh, you wouldn't know there was a reward if I hadn't told you. I'll tell you what. We'll split it. I'll give you two fifty, and I'll call the lady. That's fair, yeah?"

"Yeah, I mean, I guess, bro. Whatever."

The guard's face lights up as he pulls out his wallet. "Would you look at that? Two sixty-five in cash. Woo-hoo, perfect. Lemme make sure I got the right number and…yeah, here it is." He dials Marilyn's number. "Hey, is this Ms. Bateman? Oh, hi, this is Randy, security with Amy Beth Realtors, and I just wanted to let you know some gentleman just turned in the iPad you described." There's a pause. "Ten minutes? Okay, great. Sounds good, good-bye." Jimi can hear Marilyn's voice howling with delight. "Here ya go, two fifty."

"Thanks," says Jimi, pocketing the money and heading back to the car.

"Man, makin' two fifty is easier than stealin' candy from a baby," says Jimi as he opens the car door to the back seat. He hops in, and Kurt rushes off.

"You got the badge?" asks Kurt.

"Yep," says Marilyn, fixing her hair.

"Where's that place again?"

"Two blocks down, take a right," says Marilyn, changing from her blazer into a lace spaghetti-strap shirt, leather leggings, and platforms. "I'm not sure why I do all the work around here. I'm not cleaning if I'm doing this and going to houses later."

"We know. We'll do it," says Jimi. "Same spot? If you're not back in thirty, I'm driving back here, okay?"

"Yeah, got it. Here's good. Yep, this is the corner. Watch me work, gentlemen!" Marilyn slips out the back door, and Jimi and Kurt park around the corner. Marilyn walks to the street sign and lights a cigarette, casually leaning against it, looking for prey. Right before she's smoking the filter, an older blue Corolla stops and rolls down the window. A Latino pulls his neck over to the passenger-side window.

"Wassup, mami? What you doin', lookin' all good on that sign?"

She laughs and walks to the window. "Oh, just out here livin' the dream, you know. What you need, hun?"

"Blow job?" he asks, smiling. "How much?" He's missing two teeth and has a mole above his eye.

"Thirty."

"Hell yeah." Marilyn slips in the front seat, the car door making an immense amount of noise as she opens it. On the floor are empty beer bottles, soda cans, and a lighter.

"Pull in here, please, señor."

He doesn't say anything, just excitedly reaches for his wallet in his back pocket. Marilyn does the same, except she pulls out a police badge and flashes it at him.

"You're fucked, bro. I'm an undercover agent with the FBI and affiliated with the El Paso County Sheriff's office. You are probably going to jail for a long, long time."

"No, shut up, fuck!" he yells, plus profanity in Spanish, while he beats his fists on the steering wheel.

"Or since you seem like a nice, married man and I'm feeling rather giving today, I'll let you off easy."

"Yes, please, anything! Please just no, don't tell my wife!"

"Give me all of the cash in your wallet, and we'll forget the whole thing."

"Okay, let's see, umm…eighty-three. Is okay?"

"Yeah, whatever. Just please don't let me see you out here again, sir, and I'll be looking."

"Yes, ma'am, Officer! No, never again!"

"Mm-kay. Have a good one," says Marilyn somberly. She steps out of the Corolla and heads back to the meeting spot to find Jimi and Kurt.

"Hey! How much you get?" asks Jimi. Kurt has nodded out in the passenger seat.

"Eighty-three, boys. Shall we go to the next place?"

"Ha. Fuck yeah, good job, Mar."

"Go to that residential area. What's that neighborhood called? I got a guy over there."

"Oh, Los Salos or something?"

"Yeah, yeah. Head there."

"You got it," says Jimi, turning up the radio.

"Drive carefully. There's hella cops over here."

"Roger that," says Jimi.

Jimi slowly and cautiously ends up on the outskirts of the city in a quiet neighborhood.

"It's that one, the third to your right," says Marilyn.

"Oh, that guy? I remember him, I think."

"No, you don't. He's new."

"Aight. Same drill? You're not back in ten, I'm coming in, okay?"

The operation begins with Marilyn going into the house of a man she met online. He smiles, looking as if he hasn't showered and has been playing video games all day. Jimi snorts a line and plays *Clash of Clans* on his phone, parked down the street. He's about to attack when Marilyn jumps in the back seat.

"Go, fucker!" she screams. Jimi throws down his phone and floors the gas. The man whom Marilyn met ten minutes ago is screaming and shaking his fists in the air.

"What happened?"

"Fell for the oldest trick in the book. Told him I get paid up front but my phone must have fallen out of my pocket outside. He bought it, I ran."

"Ha! How much he give you?"

"One seventy-five."

"Damnnn, Gina," says Jimi, giving her a high five. "That's, like, five hunnid bucks today."

"Yeah, for doing next to nothing," says Marilyn, smiling and looking out the window.

"Bro, you down for *Call of Duty* at home or…" asks Kurt.

"Yeah, if Prince isn't playing it or Pac-Man in the arcade. But we just made a few hundred, but I'm running low. We'll give Ocielle the cash, get the dope, turn around, and give her pack a quarter to play for…how many hours again?"

"Shit, for a quarter? I think four hours. Plus she just got that dope-ass *Star Trek* vintage Nintendo."

"Yeah, but I'm runnin' low. Maybe she'll be all right with a dime to play? Plus Carlos isn't coming back for two days. Before we left, I heard O on the phone with Carlos talking about how she was taking too much and he couldn't get enough, real talk."

"Damn, dude, that's a problem. Wait, isn't the fight on tonight? Mayweather and Pacquiao?"

"Oh, hell yeah. Did O order it?"

"She said she would, but we'd have to pay her."

"We'll be all right. We just made five hundred in cash."

"Um, correction. *I* made five hundred," says Marilyn. "That money goes to *moi*."

Chapter 34

Intervention

"Is it even my place to intervene?" I ask Orlando at Contin Farm in the arcade, his favorite room. We start to fool around on the pool table when I have to stop to ask him the plaguing question.

"Shit, Poppy, are you serious?" he says, obviously sexually frustrated. I keep rehashing the last couple of days with the trash, the blood, the nodding out, the dead body thrown in the ground, Janis's mangled leg, the science project in a spoon, the blood, the cotton, the belted and strangled arms and body parts, the funeral. These addicts may be too far gone, if they are even sane.

"I don't think. You're not having doubts, are you? Tell me I haven't been spending all my time with junkies the past couple days for nothing," he says.

"You haven't been spending the last couple days with junkies. You've *also* been spending it with *me*," I say, smiling. He rolls his eyes.

"You're doing this intervention. These people are fucked up. You're only having doubts now because this is becoming normal to you. In the real world, people don't wear fanny packs with dope and needles in them with pride like it's a cute fuckin' thing to do." He sits next to me on the pool table. Amy walks by with a book of poetry in her hand. I don't see her much during the day, so I'm taken aback by the thought that she's been listening to us.

"Afternoon to ya," she says. We both wave.

"What are you reading?" I ask her.

"Oh, just some Walt Whitman rubbish."

"Not a bad read," I say. Amy nods and walks away, reading aloud Whitman's versus about electric things and America.

"Fuck, I hope she didn't hear us! We were whispering though, right?" I ask Orlando.

"Yes, we were. Have been the whole time. She couldn't hear anything. We hear someone come in the front door.

"What's-their-names are back. I guess they didn't get arrested," says Orlando.

"What? How'd you know where they went?" I ask.

"Prince told me. They have, like, all these different scams they do and shit to get money so Ocielle can, who knows wire money to Mexico or order another one of those hideous orange box bags with the locks I don't know. Really should be spending it on therapy."

"The fight's…in ten…minutes!" yells Kurt.

"You want it, it'll cost you!" says Ocielle.

"How much?"

"Three grams. Each. Except Marilyn. She did all the work, so she's good. Kurt and Jimi, open her up," she says, holding out her hand.

Upstairs in the theater room, Orlando tells me he needs to show me something and hands me his phone. My dad texted him and said he was about fifteen minutes away. "You need to try to bring everyone outside, but casually." Considering this would be a definite cause of suspicion, I mouth, "Any ideas?" to Orlando.

When the fight goes to a commercial, he writes in the notes of his phone: "Take one of your earrings off. Start to panic. We'll say you had them outside."

"Commercial shot break, y'all!" says Kurt, unzipping his fanny pack and slapping his veins.

I'm wearing cubic zirconia studs that can easily be real. I excuse myself, go to the bathroom, take off an earring and slide it into my pocket, and confidently head out the door.

"Oh my God, y'all! My diamond earring is gone!" I yell, holding my earlobe.

"Uh-oh! Where'd you have it last?" asks Ocielle.

"I don't know. Wait. Maybe outside? I had them both on for sure, yeah. Shit. Can y'all help me, please? Those were my grandmother's diamonds!" I say hysterically, running downstairs. I can hear Orlando trying to convince the group to help. My heart races. I'm (we're) fucked if we don't get everyone outside.

I try not to pay attention to who is coming out to help while I am on my hands and knees, looking on the ground in the midst of orange caps and syringes.

"Where were you sitting?"

"Over here. Oh gosh, I really need everyone's help!"

"Y'all get your high asses out here and help us!" yells Ocielle to the crew upstairs. A couple of minutes into the search, one by one, everyone comes out, and pretty soon Orlando, Ocielle, Amy, Marilyn, Jimi, Prince, Kurt, and I are all searching the ground for something that is hidden in my pocket.

"There…wait…I think I see it…nope, never mind," says Prince.

"That's just a pebble, Prince!" Amy yells.

"Ugh! Prince!" I say, feeling like an asshole.

"I bet the fight's…back on," I hear Jimi say to Kurt.

"No, screw the fight. Please help me. I really need to find it!" I pull tears from my eyelids to show desperation, and wipe my eyes when I spot a white van pulling in the driveway. Nobody notices, since their backs are turned. I start to panic and glance at Orlando, who hears the tires creeping. This is finally it. It's time to offer help to these diseased individuals. It's show time.

"Who the hell is that?" asks Ocielle. She starts walking backward toward the house. The others look up, suspiciously.

"No, it's okay. It's my parents. I told them…I needed a ride."

"Isn't your car right there?" she asks.

"Yeah, but it needs a new transmission. It isn't starting."

They all shield their eyes from the sun with their hands, while I try to distract them from the ambush they're about to experience. I can finally breathe deep now. If everything goes to shit, at least I tried.

"Okay, let's keep looking!" I say, unsuccessful at getting their attention.

"Are they getting out? Why are they getting out?"

"I just told them some things about a couple people here, and they were inspired to meet y'all, so…"

Orlando is eyeing the van. "Who's that?" asks Orlando. I turn around and nearly faint as Max steps out of the vehicle.

"Oh my God," I say, walking briskly to greet them and try to figure out why Max is there.

"We brought you a surprise, Poppy. He said y'all had a falling out and he hadn't heard from you, like us, because you make poor decisions sometimes." I'm speechless for a moment, and Max walks over to me, grabs my face, and kisses me hard.

"Don't fucking ever do this shit again. Do you understand me?" I kiss him back, having missed him too but having also enjoyed spending time with Orlando.

"Don't. Um, not now," I say and pull away, avoiding Orlando's reaction to what he just witnessed.

"Who the fuck is that, Poppy?" asks Orlando.

"What's up, bro? I'm Max. Her live-in boyfriend she ran out on." He extends his hand. Orlando refuses.

"Ex. He's my *ex*-boyfriend."

"Okay! Let's all come over here!" say my dad and Ryan.

"I don't know what's going on, Poppy, but don't distract from what we drove nine hours to accomplish," my dad says. I nod in agreeance, in shock and confusion. I can feel it coming. Stay the fuck away from me, go away, I repeat to myself. You're not going to dictate my life anymore.

"I need my purse, water."

"I'll get it," say Orlando and Max awkwardly at the same time.

"I got this, bro. I've been dealing with it for three days now," Orlando says to Max.

"Oh, yeah? Try two years, big shot."

"No, stop. Y'all, stop."

"Okay, what the hell is going…on up in here?" asks Prince.

"I'm glad you asked that," says the interventionist. "Let's all…can you guys all gather around so we can chat real quick? I'd really appreciate it."

"Are you a cop?" asks Kurt.

"Ha, no. The name's Ryan. I'm actually a licensed interventionist."

"Oh my God," moan Marilyn and Amy.

"What the fuck? We've been set up?" intrudes Jimi.

"What's an interventionist?" asks Ocielle. When she says that, a wave of relief washes over me.

"Hey, guys. So these are my amazing parents, and this is our friend Ryan with the iPad who wants to talk to y'all if that's…all right. And this is my ex, Max." He nods and presses his lips together.

"Why's he here? We thought…is Orlando not your lover?" asks Amy. The euphoria wafts in and out.

"Guys, I have some things to show you. Then you can ask all the questions you want about Max and Poppy and…Orlando?" Ryan looks at Orlando.

"Yeahhhhhhppp," he snips. "That's me."

"Unresolved issues saved for later. What are these things you speak of?" asks Amy.

"Just some videos," says Ryan.

Ocielle's face still remains cold, and one of suspicion.

My mother is talking to Orlando. I'm assuming he's introducing himself while Max eyes him in disgust.

"You want us to sit or…" asks Marilyn.

"Yeah, please," Ryan says, distracted by the cemetery. "So listen, guys. I've done my homework with the information Poppy's given me, and I was actually able to get in touch with some of your families." Kurt's mouth drops, Amy covers hers in shock, Jimi frowns, and Marilyn is emotionless.

"Oh my God, what the fuck, Poppy?" says Ocielle, glaring at me. "You bitch."

"Hey, hey, calm down," says Prince. "Sit down, boo-boo." He gently pulls her hand. "Let's hear him out."

"What's your name?" Ryan asks Amy.

"What is but a name? According to the government though, mine is Amy."

"Hey, Amy, I'm Ryan. I got this footage if you wanna take a look," he says, handing her the iPad.

"Oh my God, my baby!"

"Mommy, I miss you. When will you come home? We can't find you, mommy," says Rokko.

"Tell her what you're learning in school," a man's voice says in the background.

"Um…I can write my name! Look! *R-o-k-k-o*." Amy's eyes fill with tears.

"Oh my God, my baby! Hi, baby! Mommy misses you."

She trembles, almost giving the machine back.

"I painted this for you in art class. It's me and you at the park! Remember when you would take me to the park? I wish you still did, Mom. Hurry and come home, okay, Mommy!"

Amy collapses in sobs. "Why? Why did you show that to me? Where is my baby?" she screams.

"He's at home in Joplin, Missouri, with his dad. He's fine. A happy, energetic little guy you have. He also really misses his mom."

"I can't…I can't," she says, sobbing.

"Can't what?"

"Be a good-enough mother for him. I don't deserve him!"

"Of course you do, Amy. Especially now that he's getting old enough to remember things. I understand you have some legal issues with the court, Amy, but if you can stay clean, there's a highly probable chance you can regain custody of Rokko. Would you be interested in that?"

She nods silently, still crying. "I couldn't imagine wanting anything more than a mother wants her child back."

"Okay, well, let us help you get there."

"How? How am I inclined enough to be the mother he needs? I often ponder how much easier his life would be if I were dead. A longing he wouldn't have if I'd died long ago."

"All children need their mother and their father, Amy. I know you don't feel like it now, but there's hope for you. I've seen a lot worse. Now, Prince, is it? I have something to show you," Ryan says, handing him the iPad.

"All right, all right."

"Hello, Prince. Um, where in God's name are you? I'm here with *your* son, who, as you know, is disabled. His eyes don't light up anymore like he did when you were around him. We're really struggling, Prince. I'm powerless to help this baby all by myself *and* work. Vanessa's off at college, which is wonderful because she is flourishing. Luckily, the government gives Johnny a part-time caretaker a few days during the week so I can work to feed us. I've been praying hard, Prince. I ask God for your return, but…I'm losing the faith." His wife's voice cracks. "I've been praying for you to come back, but only if you're sober. I need the man I married, not some shadow of a man who shields his pain and guards his heart and feelings…with drugs. The same shit that nearly killed our son. Come back, Prince. But only if you're sober."

"Wow, Wanda." Prince closes his eyes, and tears become loose over his cheeks.

"Your wife?" asks Ryan.

"Yeah. I swear to God I want to come home, but I know I'm stuck on this nasty roller coaster from hell, and I just can't get off. I just can't. Believe you me, I've tried, I've tried, you know? I just can't. For some reason I can't kick this shit. I've been in the military, done some intense shit. But I can't stay off the drugs."

"Absolutely. I know a hundred percent, Prince, what you're going through—well, all of you—because I've been there too."

"You have?"

"Yep. I was another hopeless addict living on the streets in South Dallas. One night when I was panhandling, a driver gave me a book. I nodded, pretending to be grateful, but addicts aren't really grateful beings by nature. Honestly, I was pissed. I needed money to score dope, not read a damn book! I had the reading comprehension of a sixth grader, but I kept the silly pamphlet anyway. Three weeks later I finally read it on a boring evening. It was a minibook about the twelve steps of Alcoholics Anonymous."

"I mean, I had a full life before this shit," says Prince. "I had a wife, two beautiful kids who just, I think…made it through her first semester of college. She got a full ride."

"Yeah? That's awesome, but I bet they'd really like to have their dad back. How long have you been using?"

"Shit, heroin? I think a few years now, but I don't shoot it. Just sniff. And you know it was all because of a dentist? The next day after a filling, my jaw was in some awful state. I called her up, you know, like, 'What's good, lady? My jaw hurts like a motherfucker.' She says, 'I'll call you in a narcotic if it doesn't get better soon.' After I got that first pill, man, I tell you what: I wanted to feel like that always. It was what I'd been missing."

Prince's eyes light up like bottle rockets. He tells us it's orgasmic, euphoric, like a warm, fuzzy, tingly, safe blanket, until it sucks your soul dry and you lose everything you ever had. "You know, I had it all. Nice house, three stories, my wife and I both drove Range Rovers, and we worked hard and had both of my kids' college tuition saved, but…"

"You spent it?"

"Yep. Now there's medical bills for my disabled son, who overdosed and didn't die, praise Jesus, but it destroyed his brain, his functioning, due to a few seconds of oxygen loss."

"That's awful, Prince. I'm sorry for that loss," says Ryan, cupping his chin with his hand.

"Yeah, I knew the shit could kill you, but I had never heard it can leave you vegetated."

"Oh my, I'm so sorry to hear about that, Prince, sincerely. But you can show up for him now. He still needs you, and what about your daughter? She deserves her father back. Do you think you have an addiction problem?"

"I'd suppose so…sometimes."

"What, then, is holding you back from going home?"

"Oh, you mean gettin' clean?"

"Yes."

"Well, shit, I dunno, man. I'm not one for no withdrawals. I may be six two, but I am *not* a good withdrawaler. The pain takes me back every time."

"We have things we'll give you to ease the symptoms, but these are only *short-term remedies*. It's not our intention—and I say this to everyone—to get you off heroin but simultaneously hooked on Suboxone. I've seen it happen too many times, where addicts are replacing one drug with another, and it doesn't work like that."

"How does it work?" asks Marilyn.

"It reduces the symptoms, but it's still a narcotic. If you're serious about your sobriety, then there doesn't need to be any hesitation about going for it and pushing through a couple bad days of withdrawal. In treatment, we don't serve alcoholics beer to ease their hard-alcohol addiction. We just get them to a modified level where they're comfortable."

"How?"

"Alcoholic withdrawals cause seizures, so we need to make sure our patients are safe with antiseizure meds. Heroin withdrawals make you *feel* like you're dying but don't have the power to actually kill you. We have things for heroin withdrawal, but it's only a short-term remedy for a couple days to get you through the worst of the withdrawals. See, guys, the issue isn't detoxing you from withdrawals. That's easy. A lot of people in this field believe removing the withdrawal symptoms will get and keep addicts clean. It doesn't."

"Wait, who are you again?" asks Jimi.

"This is my dad, Hugo. He owns a rehab facility in Dallas," I say.

"Wait, what the fuck? You really did set us up?" asks Jimi.

"Well, no, not exactly—"

"Oh, yeah? Then inform us all what you call it," says Amy.

"Look, I didn't come here intending on intervening in your lives. I just ended up here on a whim and wanted to do my part as someone in recovery, especially since my dad works at a treatment facility."

"The addict's real issue is a spiritual malady, or lack of a spiritual connection to a power greater than yourself. Heroin, alcohol, money, or whatever the drug are the only *tools* addicts have to deal with life. Jimi, I have something for you," says Ryan, handing him the iPad. We hear an older man's voice speaking.

"Hey, Jimbo. I sincerely hope this finds you. Your mother and I miss you terribly, and you need to come home or to accept the treatment plan being offered to you. I'm so sorry you feel like we abandoned you. That was never my, your mom's, or your siblings' intention."

Then we hear a young woman's voice crying in distress and desperation. "We want our brother back, Jimi. Please take the help. Please still be alive and watching this. Do the right thing, please. We can't take not knowing where our missing brother is anymore." Jimi's face stays the same, a look of shock and confusion. It ends with a small crowd of people saying, "We miss you, love you, Jambalaya!"

"Your family seems like some cool people," says Ryan. Jimi doesn't respond, only shrugs like a sour teenager. "Can you hand it to Marilyn, please? Her video is next, I believe." Jimi obeys, and we hear a woman's voice.

"Oh my God, Mom," Marilyn says.

"Hi, baby. I was just informed that you weren't actually at a treatment center, that you were still using. How could you do this to me?"

"Wow, she's gained weight," says Marilyn. Ryan rolls his eyes.

"As you can tell, I've been overemotional eating, but I've been seeing this guy for a few months. You'd really like him. Please come back to Los Angeles, Marilyn, where you belong. Get the help you need so you can come back and we can be a family again."

"Mitchell!" says Marilyn, seeing her dog.

"Aw, you hear Mitchy? He says he wants you to come home too." Mitchell barks. Marilyn laughs. I haven't seen her laugh since we got here. I really didn't think she had it in her.

"Ugh, my dog, you guys. God, I miss him." No one mentions anything about her not mentioning her mother.

"Hey! That's my mom!" says Kurt, snatching the device away.

"Yeah, they all roll together," says Ryan.

"Hey, Kurty. Where are you? Please just let me know if you're okay!" A woman is howling through the speakers.

"I'm fine, Momma."

"Kurt, your mom hasn't been herself since you've disappeared again. Please just let us know you're safe. Your face has been all over the news almost religiously for a year. When we got word that someone might have located you, I saw your mom smile again for the first time in over a year. Come on, son. Let us know you're safe, accept the treatment you're being offered, and come home again. We love you."

"We love you!" we hear his mom say in the background. Kurt's eyes have filled with tears.

"I can't take this shit. This is too much," says Marilyn, getting dope from her fanny pack.

Ocielle yawns and says how bored she is, when her phone starts to ring. She looks at the number in a panic and runs inside.

Chapter 35

The Question

Inside Contin Farm kitchen

"Hey! What's up? Are you going to be coming out here soon? I need more. There's a doctor or someone here trying to get them off drugs! I need you out here ASAP to lure them back in. Carlos, please tell me you're coming!"

"Hey, mami, no, no, I won't. I'm calling you from a correctional facility in New Mexico. I got fucking pulled over."

"Oh my God, did you have any, a lot in the car?" she asks frantically. No Carlos means no heroin, and no heroin means no friends, no Contin Farm, no nothing. She will be alone again. She hyperventilates, having thoughts about being a lonely little girl again, playing alone in her room.

"Cops said they found about twenty ounces total, but I can dispute that, I bet."

"Oh my God. What are you going to do? What am *I* going to do?" she asks, tears starting to blur her vision when she remembers the promise she made to herself about never going back to that isolated little girl. She needs Sadie.

"What are *you* going to do? You're not the one taking the bait here. But listen, I really need a favor, baby. My bail is set for a half a million right now."

"Okay, what you want me to do about that?"

"Call Santiago."

The thought of speaking to her dad again makes her freeze. "Are you fucking kidding me? A, he won't talk to me, and B, even if you *did* get bailed out, you lost him, what, twenty grand, Carlos? He's literally going to slaughter you."

"Oh my God, I know. Can you ask him? Please, Ocielle, I have a daughter to feed."

She recalls the last time she and her father spoke, almost two years ago. They'd just gotten into another fight over her boyfriend at the time, Mark. Santiago didn't like the fact that Mark was white and was convinced that he was hired to spy on Santiago and his family, using Ocielle as a prop. She was in love, but Daddy didn't believe him. He wrote Ocielle a check for $1.1 million and told her she could have the house in West Texas and the three acres of land surrounding it but that it needed to be renovated. It was all hers as long as she and Mark got the hell out of his life. Those words haunted her every night for the past two years. She was unable to shake it. She and Mark broke up shortly after, since he wasn't a fan of the sometimes painfully slow West Texas pace, when soon after she met Amy in El Paso at a grocery store and started talking. Amy had a sign saying that she was homeless and needed money, so Ocielle recommended she come live with her.

When Ocielle discovered Amy was an addict, she told her that she could order drugs for her and they'd be there in a day or two, if she agreed to stay at Contin Farm and live with her. Shortly after, Prince made his way, then a plethora of random junkies who have since left or died.

"Let me ask y'all this. Raise your hand if you have a relationship with a higher power," says Ryan.

No one raises a hand. Prince comments that he used to but God didn't like him because he was making him so miserable and not answering his prayers.

"What's needed is a relationship with a God of *your own* understanding who removes the urge to use once you get honest with yourself and do a few things."

The sun is starting to set, but no one notices its sharp magnificence. Orlando is carelessly leaning back on his hands, closing his eyes from time to time. Max has decided to wait in the van, resisting the urge to kill Orlando.

"Yeah, well, for me it's the whole God thing. That and the fact that I wasn't homeless or living under a bridge or panhandling," says Jimi.

"Like, what the fuck has God ever done for *me*? I feel like in the past I've gone to church, I've done the things, but was never able to really get it. You know what I mean?" asks Kurt.

"Yes, of course," says Ryan, excited. "Totally. Thank you both for being honest, but let me ask you this: What have you done for God or other people? And Jimi, most people think you need to fill certain requirements in order to qualify as an addict, when it's simply a moment of clarity when you comprehend that you can't stop on your own terms once you start, even if you've only lost control once. Normal drinkers or normal heroin users can do it once and say, 'Thanks, that's cool, but no more,' and get on with their lives. They always maintain a sense of control *and* enjoyment simultaneously. Addicts and alcoholics can't do that. If they're enjoying it, they're not controlling it, and if they're controlling it, they don't enjoy it."

"Fuck this shit. You guys don't have a problem. If y'all *really* had a problem or were addicts, you'd be on the street, living under a bridge, but you're not. You're in a fucking mansion with an indoor pool," says Ocielle, walking back outside from the kitchen.

"So Ocielle, you think these guys aren't addicts, because they live in a nice house?"

"If the removal of drugs and alcohol was the only thing you had to do, you would've all been sober a long time ago, right?" Asks Ryan.

Ryan proceeds to ask how many people have tried to get sober on their own. Everyone raises a hand.

What destroys the addict is the normal day-to-day life. People who are not addicts and not alcoholics don't seem to grasp that this is the reality of addicts, and it's not simply the removal of drugs and alcohol from the system that solves the problem.

"Please save that for later, if you don't mind," says Ryan, looking at Amy starting to melt contents into a spoon.

"That I will do." She smiles. "And when were you expecting to depart?"

"Really though, guys, listen. I won't be trying to convince you that you're an alcoholic or drug addict or that you *should* get sober. I'm not a doctor or a saint. I just want to help guide you to your truth of what being an addict means, and the options you have if you wish to recover. Unfortunately, though it seems impossible, the removal of heroin is the easy part. Where the tough get going is staying sober and maintaining the capability to be a sober, functioning human being in the real world. Ask yourself, do you really want to change? Not for your family or friends, but for yourself. You have to want to become a different person, a better person. This is the only way the steps will work for you. What brought you to Contin Farm, Amy?" Ryan asks.

"The court system took my child away. Ripped from my arms in the night, so I fled. I was transient in El Paso at the time when I met Ocielle, who really saved me. After all, the law took my flesh, my heart, and…my soul. I am nothing without him."

"Do you think you have a heroin addiction?"

"Some days, yes, some days…maybe not. I've used other narcotics, however, and didn't have the interest in them like the pills, so I didn't consider myself a *drug* addict. I'm just a confused soul. I am out at night with lanterns, looking for myself. I have indeed made some bad decisions and am just fickle, fickle, fickle…always changing my mind."

"Did it ever occur to you, or to you guys, that *you* weren't actually changing your mind but that instead the decision was made for you?"

"By whom?"

"Your disease. Your disease wants you dead, all of you. You can continue to live in disbelief and think you have control, but if you do, why didn't you get things under control before the court system yanked your kid away? Surely you would have quit before then, if you had all the control and power, right?"

"Whatever. You have the power," snaps Ocielle. "You make your own mind up to do heroin, and whatever else you want. You have all the control, no matter what this guy says. You are the master of your own fate. The captain of your own damn soul. Everyone is." I slice Ocielle apart with my stare.

"I suppose…what if…I don't have the control then? Maybe, sir, you are right," says Amy.

My dad once told me that pain-management specialists are nothing other than glorified drug dealers. Sure, it's the addicts who swallow the pills, who are the ones primarily at fault, but when giving something as potent as fentanyl, morphine, or OxyContin to someone with a weak moral compass (or none at all), it's almost certainly to turn into a disaster. It's happening all over the world. OxyContin and its counterparts should be reserved for those in end-of-life pain or for those recovering from *major* surgery. Even then, a single handful should suffice. Any more than that, and a good majority are off to the races. Then they run out of funds, and someone says, "Hey, try heroin. It's cheaper." What happens next is the fear of withdrawal and the never-ending chase for more.

Ask any alcoholics or drug addicts why they do what they do, and they offer any number of excuses. These excuses range from "Because my husband had an affair" to the weather, "My kid was killed in an accident ten years ago," "I'm an anxious person," and so on. If all these "problems" addicts and alcoholics say they drink/use over were removed, they would still find a reason to justify their drinking or using. At the end of the day, addicts and alcoholics *do not know* why they drink the amount they do or why they stick needles in their arms.

"Guys, this isn't going to be easy, and I'm not here to convince you of something if you don't know yourself. Addiction is a confusing epidemic. It's the only disease those who are affected by don't believe they have. Despite all sorts of voices from friends, doctors, and employers," starts Hugo, "you will never find anyone who was diagnosed with colon cancer exiting the doctor's office, denying they actually have cancer and therefore they don't need to follow a chemo regimen because it's inconvenient, the doctor's a quack, even though they have all of the symptoms and the test results are positive. Unless you're clinically insane, you'd leave the doctor with a solid, consistent treatment plan and steps for your recovery. Whatever they may be, you're willing to do it to get well, right?" Almost everyone nods. "You would take the doctor's advice because you know that to be free of any ailment, it requires you to do a few things."

"Marilyn, what do you think's keeping you from getting sober? Your mom told us how you told her you were already doing so. Can you tell me a little of your story and relationship?" asks Ryan.

"Well, I don't know. Our relationship…is rocky. Like, for instance, she told me I needed a nose job, so I did that…and when…I was sixteen…she gave me these kinds of pills for the rhinoplasty pain. After I took one, I didn't feel much, but after the third dose a couple days later, I was more talkative and giddy than ever before. I didn't realize how addicted I became until the pills ran out. I found myself digging in my mom's medicine cabinet for these magic pills called Percocets but couldn't find any. I had a girlfriend of mine who told me about becoming a sugar baby so these men would pay for my stuff if I slept with them. So I signed up."

"And your mom?"

"Oh, she doesn't know. She's more concerned with herself…I mean, you saw it. She's supposed to be telling me how much she loves and misses me, and she's talking about her fucking boy toy, after she's learned her daughter is still using and not in rehab like she thought."

"Look, I know you think you were maybe trying to help her or put her mind at ease by lying, but secrets keep people sick. Listen, we have a great program back in Dallas, and we surprisingly have beds available at no cost to you—"

"For how long?" asks Jimi.

"For what?" says Hugo.

"Will we have to stay for?"

"However long it takes, Jimi. Some people forty-five days, others over a year."

"Fuck that."

"Oh, okay. Then your option is to…"

"Stay here with Ocielle, work, get high."

"Actually…I don't know what's going to happen, guys," Ocielle says, crying. We all immediately turn toward her. "Carlos got arrested in El Paso."

"What the fuck!" shouts Marilyn.

"But that doesn't mean you guys can't get dope. I'll find a way. Just please stick with me!"

"Oh, okay, so the dealer is gone. That means everyone here will be back on the streets, so you might as well get clean," says Ryan, smiling.
"Fuck you. Don't you *know* who I *am*? I can get my friends drugs!" Ocielle shouts. Ryan stays quiet, making a "good luck" face.

"Did she really just say that?" says Orlando.

"Okay, enough, guys. Listen. I just need to know who here, after seeing your loved ones and after finding out you will most likely be back out on the streets, who here is ready to make the biggest and best change of their lives? Who's really had enough, for good and all?"

The silence is so loud it's deafening.